Also by Claire Boston

<u>The Texan Quartet</u>
What Goes on Tour
All that Sparkles
Under the Covers
Into the Fire

<u>The Flanagan Sisters</u>
Break the Rules
Change of Heart
Blaze a Trail
Place to Belong

Blaze a Trail

The Flanagan Sisters # 3

Claire Boston

BANTILLY PUBLISHING

First published by Bantilly Publishing in 2016

Blaze a Trail: The Flanagan Sisters 3

EPUB format: 978-0-9945528-6-0
Mobi format: 978-0-9945528-7-7
Print-on-demand format: 978-0-9945528-8-4

Cover design by Amygdala Design
Edited by Dianne Blacklock
Proofread by Grammar Smith Editing Services

DEDICATION

To my brothers-in-law, Torben and Howell

Chapter 1

The buzz of people talking about the symposium was music to Zita Flanagan's ears. She smiled. The subject of immigration was definitely a hot topic and one that needed discussing. She took a glass of red wine from the passing waiter and moved toward her mother, who was chatting with a group of migrant advocates.

"The presenters were a bunch of bleeding hearts, believing all the lies they're told." The complaint was loud, with a strong Texan drawl just off to Zita's right.

Her skin tightened and her eyes narrowed. *Keep moving.* It wouldn't do any good to get into an argument with someone like him. Especially not after she was on a high from hearing her sister's impassioned speech about the plight of Central American refugees.

As she walked by the man, he stepped back, bumping into her and she almost spilled her wine.

"Excuse me, Missy." A hand reached out to steady her and she turned to the broad-shouldered man who had more gray than brown in his hair.

Missy? Who the hell called anyone *Missy* these days? "Don't worry about it." She moved forward when he spoke again.

"You look like a sensible American gal. What do you think about the information presented at this here symposium?"

Zita grinned. People often mistook her for an American

because she took after her Irish father with her strawberry blond hair, though her skin was the color of a summer's tan. "Actually, I'm a migrant from El Salvador," she said, enjoying the way the man's eyes widened in surprise. "I believe the information presented was informative and accurate, and I can't see how anyone could possibly disagree with it, unless they were a racist bigot."

The man huffed out a breath of outrage and his face went red.

"Bob, everyone's entitled to their opinion," a deep voice said, his tone friendly.

She glanced at the man standing next to Bob. *Hello, gorgeous.* Blue eyes, the color of a tropical lagoon, blond hair styled with gel, and the sexiest smile she'd ever seen.

"I knew there'd come a day when I couldn't tell a foreigner from an American. They're learning to blend in." Bob turned to his companion for backup.

That ticked Zita off. That his comment touched one of her insecurities was like prodding a nest of vipers.

"Dad." The word was a censure coming from the sexy blond. They were related? What a shame.

"Do you agree with him too?" Zita asked, her heartbeat accelerating. "Do you think we should build a wall, stop these refugees from entering the United States, turn our backs on the people fleeing for their lives and searching for somewhere safe to live?" She was annoyed at herself for getting so worked up. There was no point talking to these people. They were too closed off in their bigotry. She moved away.

"Wait." The blond grabbed her arm to stop her and red wine flew out of her glass over his white shirt.

Zita's anger immediately dissipated. "I'm sorry." She winced. There was no point dabbing at it, it was already spreading. His shirt was ruined.

"Totally my fault," he replied, with a smile that didn't slow her heart rate.

"Goddamn it, David. I can't take you anywhere," Bob said.

David chuckled, not at all perturbed. "Let me clean myself up, and then I'd like to talk with you."

She frowned. It was doubtful that she'd want to hear what

he had to say, or that he would be able to find her again in this crowd, so she said, "Sure." Then she went to find her mother.

***

After cleaning his shirt the best he could, David walked back into the crowded ballroom, scanning the room. The attractive strawberry blonde who'd spilled wine on him was easy on the eyes, and he could use the excuse of wanting to know more about the refugee situation to start a conversation. He smiled. At first glance he couldn't see the woman, but his father beckoned him over.

Bob was talking with his friend, Governor Jesse Harding. "David, listen to this. Jesse's going to be retiring and he wants me to run for governor."

"Your father would be an excellent candidate," Jesse said.

Huh. David frowned. "What about the company? It can't run without you."

"Well, you're almost ready to take over Dionysus anyway. Could give me a new challenge."

"We need a strong leader to deal with the issue of immigration," Jesse said. "You heard the problems today."

"Something definitely needs to be done," David agreed. "I was going to speak with the woman who spilled wine on me."

"Good idea. See if you can find her. We need to gather as much information about the issues as possible," Bob said.

David pursed his lips. Minutes ago, Bob had been complaining about the bias of the symposium and the bleeding hearts, and now he wanted to help? Perhaps Jesse had explained the problems. Well, David wasn't going to miss the opportunity to find the woman again. He nodded at his father and Jesse and moved into the crowd.

It didn't take him long to see that there were far more people in the ballroom than he'd realized. He circled the room twice, keeping an eye out for his friend Carolina, who had been one of the speakers, as well as the mystery woman. Finally, he caught a glimpse of strawberry blond hair through the crowd. *There you are.* He definitely wanted more than just information from her. She was talking with a short, Hispanic lady and a slightly taller woman, whose red hair was tied up in a bun. David approached the group.

"Sure. Send me a date and time and we'll be there," the strawberry blonde was saying.

The people she was talking with smiled at him and the woman turned. She really was stunning. Her chocolate brown eyes widened as she recognized him.

"Excuse me for interrupting," David said. "May I speak with . . ." He faltered. "Sorry, I didn't catch your name earlier."

"Zita."

He smiled. "Zita. Could I have a word?"

The other women were both grinning.

She nodded and took a couple of steps away from the group. "You managed to salvage your shirt."

"I did the best I could," he said. "I don't recommend a small basin and a hand dryer as a regular washing regime." He winked.

Zita laughed. "No, I can't imagine it would be very efficient. What did you want to talk to me about?"

He paused. He didn't want to upset her again. "You seem to know a lot about the Central American immigration issue. Before I got here, all I knew was what I'd read in the newspapers."

"What made you come today?"

"My father was coming and I discovered a friend of mine was speaking. I wanted to hear what she had to say."

"Who's your friend?"

"Carolina Flanagan."

Zita stared at him. "You know Carly?"

He paused at the familiarity with which Zita spoke about Carolina. "We go way back. She's my partner in crime at all the gala events. She makes them bearable."

"You're David Randall?"

Surprised she knew his name, he nodded.

"Carly's mentioned you."

"How do you know her?"

"She's my sister."

"Of course. Small world." He should have realized. Carly often talked about her two sisters, and he'd met Bridget a few months earlier when he'd discovered she worked at one of Dionysus's oil refineries. But Zita didn't look like either of them.

"Isn't it?" she agreed.

"I was hoping to catch up with Carly this evening, but I haven't seen her."

"You won't," Zita said. "She had to fly to New York straight after her talk. Her partner has an exhibition opening tonight."

"That's great." He needed to get back on track. "Carly spoke about her charity, Casa Flanagan. I guess you'd know a lot about it."

"Yes. I work there."

"So you foster kids who have been allowed to stay in the country?"

She nodded. "But we're also participating in a trial to foster children who are waiting for their applications to be processed. Studies have shown that detention centers suck, in particular for kids. They feel trapped, isolated, and scared of what is going to happen to them. We've got three girls with us at the moment who are part of this trial."

"Who makes the decision?"

"The immigration court."

"How do they decide?"

"One way is for the girls to prove they're in danger if they go home."

"And are they?" From what he knew, the immigrants from Central America were looking for a free ride and preferred the States to their home countries.

Fire sparked in her eyes. "Yes."

"How do you know?" He was curious.

"Because they've told us their stories. Two girls are fleeing from gang violence and one girl is running from her abusive stepfather."

"Do they have proof?"

"Not usually." She glared at him. "When they're running for their lives, they don't usually stop to take evidence."

The sarcasm was clear. "Of course." David smiled agreeably, not wanting to upset her further. "How can you tell they're telling the truth?"

"I've seen their pain and their fear. I've heard their stories. They're not lying."

"So it comes down to their word?" Perhaps she was a naïve bleeding heart.

"Not always." Her hands were on her hips and her face was flushed. "We get affidavits and gather what information we can. If you want to learn, you should follow a case. Contact a detention center, talk to a child and take the journey with them through the process. Then you'll understand."

She looked like a blond Wonder Woman — sexy, assertive and defiant. "All right." The more information he had, the better he could help his father if he decided to run for governor.

She blinked. "Sorry?"

"It's a good idea. I want to learn more about the topic, and following a case makes sense." And it gave him a legitimate reason to see her again. "You said you had a couple of girls still waiting for their application. Could I follow one of those?"

Zita hesitated for a moment. "OK. We're preparing Teresa and Beatriz for their hearings soon."

"Great. Let me get your number." He pulled out his phone and typed in her details as she dictated, and then sent her a text so she had his. "I'll look forward to your call."

Zita nodded, looking a little suspicious.

"I'll let you get back to your conversation." He smiled and then walked away, knowing she was staring at him.

***

A week later, Zita drove the familiar route to the immigration lawyer's office where they would meet with Shelly. Teresa was silent next to her. At fifteen, Teresa was the oldest of the girls waiting for her application to be processed, and had been in the country for a couple of months. During that time, she'd opened up about why she'd fled El Salvador and Zita's heart bled for her. There was no way the government should send her back, but there was never any guarantee. She hoped David would realize that when he heard Teresa's story.

"Today's about getting the details down," Zita told Teresa again in Spanish. "Tell us everything and Shelly will highlight what you'll need to tell the judge."

The girl nodded, her hands clenched so tightly her knuckles were white.

Zita sighed and parked the car. "Remember David will be there, but ignore him. He's there to listen and no one to be afraid of." She hoped having David there wouldn't cause any problems, but she could always send him away.

She'd called Carly after meeting David and interrogated her about him. Though he didn't seem as antagonistic as Bob, she couldn't risk it. If he was in any way hostile, she wouldn't let him anywhere near one of her girls. Carly had vouched that he was a nice guy. He worked in finance at Dionysus Oil and Gas and had been a constant support to Carly while she was finding her feet in the business world. Carly considered him a friend. That was enough for Zita.

They walked into the immigration lawyer's office together and Zita's attention was immediately caught by David sitting in the waiting room. He was dressed in a suit again, navy blue this time, and his smile caused her heart to speed up. He was sexier than anyone had a right to be. She acknowledged him and greeted the receptionist.

"Hi Latisha, can you tell Shelly we're here?"

"Sure, Zita. She won't be long. Take a seat."

The waiting room had seats around its perimeter with only a few occupants at this time of the morning. In the middle was a coffee table with old magazines spread over it. Zita walked over to David and sat down. "David, this is Teresa. You'll be following her case over the next few months."

"Nice to meet you, Teresa." He held out his hand to the girl.

Teresa glanced at Zita, and at her encouragement, she shook it. "Hello." She quickly let go and sat on the other side of Zita.

It was no surprise the girl was skittish. Her trust in men had been lost when her father had handed her over to the local gang.

Worried Teresa might not open up with David there, Zita said, "You should just listen today. Save any questions you have until after the session."

"Sure. I don't want to cause any problems."

"Zita, Teresa, won't you come in?" Shelly was a short, red-haired woman who had been working in immigration for a decade. As always, she wore jeans and a shirt so as not to appear too imposing to her clients.

Zita stood and gestured for Teresa and David to follow.

When they reached the meeting room, Zita made the introductions and they all sat.

"As we discussed after your master calendar hearing, this next hearing is where you get to give the full details of your case."

Shelly explained the whole process. Zita had heard it all before, but she watched for signs that Teresa didn't understand, and translated for her when needed.

"Do you have any questions?" Shelly asked.

"If I am accepted, can my mother and sister come too?" Her voice was soft, but hopeful.

Zita exchanged a glance with the lawyer. They'd discussed this already.

"As soon as you've been approved, we'll put in a refugee/asylee relative petition," Shelly said. "If we can contact your mother in the meantime, we'll get her to apply for refugee status at the US consulate in San Salvador."

They'd tried contacting Teresa's mother Johanna several times over the past few months, but each time, Teresa's father had answered the phone and wouldn't allow Zita to speak with her.

"We'll keep trying," Zita said.

"There are no guarantees, Teresa," Shelly said. "But we are doing everything we can to get your family out of El Salvador."

David frowned. Quietly Zita said, "I'll explain later."

He nodded.

"Tell me your story, Teresa," Shelly continued and Teresa began to speak in Spanish with Zita translating.

"I lived in a poor suburb in San Salvador. *Mara Principal* is influential there, but they never showed much interest in my family. Mama works in a laundry and Papa does construction. As long as they paid their dues to the gang, we were left alone. Until I turned fifteen." She took a breath. "I was at the laundry waiting for my sister to come back from her friend's house and one of the gang members came in to take the weekly payment. He wanted me to go outside with him and meet his friends. I knew what would happen if I did, so I refused."

"What would happen?" Shelly asked.

"They would rape me. There was a group who would often

stop a girl who was by herself and have their way with her." She said it with no emotion at all. As if it was of no consequence.

David cleared his throat and Zita shot him a warning look to be quiet.

"Then what happened?" Shelly asked.

"The man got angry. Said I would be sorry for refusing him, and left." Teresa took a small sip of water, her hand shaking. "Two days later, Papa was fired. The foreman said the gang had made him do it. Then they put up the rent on our house. We couldn't afford to live there anymore." Her voice was full of sorrow. "Mama wasn't earning enough from the laundry and we had nowhere to live and very little food. No one would help us for fear of what the gang would do to them."

"Go on," Shelly encouraged.

"One day, one of the gang members came to my father. He said if Papa gave me to the gang, he would get his job and house back. Mama begged Papa to move, to find somewhere safe to live, but he was too scared. Papa agreed to hand me over."

Zita wanted to castrate him. How could he betray his daughter like that?

"What did the gang want with you?"

Teresa stared down at the table. "They wanted me for sex," she whispered. "The gang has a group of girls, they call them their girlfriends, but they're not really. They give the girls to men as a reward for a job well done and sometimes they sell them to men too." Teresa clenched her fist.

Zita squeezed the girl's hand.

"What happened when you went to the gang?"

Teresa glanced at David and then back to the lawyer.

"I can leave," David said.

Teresa shook her head. "It does not matter. I will have to tell my story many times." She took a deep breath. "The first day I was there, the man who started it all, the man who'd come to the laundry, forced himself on me. Then he gave me to his friends." Her voice was dull, but she clutched Zita's hand as if it were a lifeline. "After that, they sold me to men as punishment for refusing them at the beginning. I had to have sex with all of these men and if they complained about my response, I was beaten."

Tears stung Zita's eyes. She'd heard Teresa's story before, but it didn't make it any easier.

"I couldn't stay there. I had to get away. After one beating, my arm was broken. I was taken to a doctor to get it set and I managed to escape. I ran away, as far as I could and then kept going. I didn't know how far the gang's influence spread and I was too scared to stop. Then I met some others who were going to the United States and I joined them. It was better than staying in El Salvador."

Shelly continued to ask questions, getting more details from the girl. Zita looked at David. His jaw was set and the steely look in his eyes was formidable. She was reassured that Teresa's story had affected him.

It took several hours for Shelly to record the information, and to update them on the intel they'd received from El Salvador. Fernando, their contact there, was trying to fight the gangs from inside the country. He was investigating how to shut down the sex slave rings, but it was a dangerous job.

"Why can't he speak with my mother?" Teresa asked, tears welling in her eyes.

"Johanna refused to talk to him," Zita told her again. "It's hard to know who to trust."

Teresa burst into tears and Zita pulled her close. "We're trying, *niñita*." Her words were inadequate, but there was little else she could do. She glanced at Shelly, who looked as sad as Zita felt.

"A hearing date has been set for January," Shelly told them. "We'll go over the details again before then."

Zita shook the woman's hand. "Thank you."

Teresa wiped her eyes and they walked out of the building. The girl climbed straight into Zita's yellow SUV, but Zita turned to David. "I'm sorry, any questions you've got will have to wait. I need to get Teresa home." She couldn't deal with him now. Not when Teresa needed her and her heart was raw.

He nodded and ran a hand down her arm. She closed her eyes briefly, allowing herself to be soothed, surprised he was being so kind.

"Can I call you later?"

"Sure." She'd like to hear what he thought, whether any of

his preconceptions had been challenged. She got into her car, pushing further thoughts of David aside. She felt so helpless when she sat in the meetings, listening to Shelly plan their case. There was nothing she could do, except be there for Teresa, and that wasn't enough. She was tired of waiting for things to happen and being the passive attendee. She wanted to fight for her foster sisters, to develop their cases and to secure their freedom. What she really wanted was to be a lawyer.

But it could never happen. Her mother needed her too much at Casa Flanagan. She didn't have the time to study.

Besides, she hadn't been a great student at high school anyway. She probably wouldn't even get into college.

It was all just a pipe dream. One she should probably forget.

With a sigh, she drove Teresa home.

***

Zita drove away and David ran a hand over his face. He wasn't sure what he'd been expecting when he'd attended the meeting today, but it sure as hell wasn't that. His stomach was tied up in knots, and he'd been nauseated as the girl had told her story.

There was little doubt in his mind that she was telling the truth.

But neither Zita nor Shelly had seemed surprised by it. Was it a common story, or had they heard it before and had a chance to take it all in?

He walked back into the office, hoping to get some answers. Shelly was talking with her receptionist.

"David, did you forget something?"

"No. Do you have a couple of minutes to answer some questions? Zita had to get Teresa home."

"If you're quick." She led him into her office and sat down. "What do you want to know?"

"How common is Teresa's story?"

"Teresa's is one of the worst I've heard in a while, but sexual assault is common among the girls who arrive. If they weren't abused before they left home, they are often abused by the traffickers bringing them here."

He felt sick. "Do many get sent back home?"

She nodded. "It depends on the judge and how clear their case is. Most of these kids don't think about bringing evidence with them, they very rarely even have money. They just run. Those who are looking for a better life, but have no real problems at home, aside from the usual poverty, generally get sent back. Those like Teresa, who have a true asylum case take longer to process and we have a good success rate with them."

"But it's not one hundred percent?"

"No. Unfortunately."

He couldn't understand it. How could anyone listen to Teresa's story and not grant her asylum?

Shelly glanced at her watch.

He'd taken enough of her time. "Thank you."

"You're welcome."

David walked out and stood under cover in the entrance, watching the rain that was falling in sheets. It was a miserable gray day, and it suited his mood.

How did Zita cope hearing the girls' stories? It was gut-wrenching, and the girls must need counseling. He was a little shell-shocked himself. He'd been friends with Carly for years, and had never known the kind of work she was involved in. Was he completely self-absorbed?

He had a good life. His family was high on the ridiculously wealthy scale, and he'd never gone without. He ran a hand through his hair. He wanted time to process what he'd learned, do some research of his own, check statistics and start putting together some details, but he was due at work.

Exhaling, he tried to clear his jumbled thoughts. He'd take this opportunity to learn about immigration and about those less fortunate than himself. Hopefully he'd be able to help in some way.

Pleased with his decision, he dashed out to his car.

Chapter 2

The last thing Zita felt like doing was going out. She was exhausted from the session with Shelly, and Teresa was still upset. But she'd promised her friend Rebecca weeks ago that she would go out with her cousin. She hated blind dates, but Rebecca knew which buttons to push. Give her a sob story and Zita always tried to make it better. Sometimes she wished she wasn't so empathetic.

She should give the guy a chance. He might be great.

She dressed quickly, choosing flared red jeans and a knitted aqua sweater, and then hurried downstairs to check if her mother needed any help with dinner. Zita disliked going out on a weeknight because she was leaving her with too much work with the six foster girls.

"Mama, can I help with anything?" she asked, walking into the kitchen.

"You look gorgeous, *niñita*," Carmen said as she stirred a pot, the rich smells of beef and beans wafting out. "I've got this covered. You don't want to spill anything on your top."

"You sure?" She took a seat at the breakfast bar.

"Of course. Now, we haven't had a chance to talk about where you're going tonight."

Zita sighed. She should have known the inquisition was coming. "It's a blind date with Rebecca's cousin. I think we're going to the steakhouse."

"Can't he find his own woman?"

Zita smiled. "He's just moved to Houston and doesn't know many people."

"So you're expected to show him a good time?" Carmen raised an eyebrow.

"It's only dinner."

"What happened with the lovely David?"

"David?" His name made her more alert. "He's only interested in learning more about the immigration issue." Which was kind of a shame. He was very attractive and she'd like to spend more time with him.

"Really? A gorgeous man like that not interested in my baby? Is he gay?"

Zita coughed. "I don't know. We've only spoken a couple of times."

Her dogs, Bess and Saint, started barking at the front door. Relieved to end the conversation, Zita got to her feet. "That will be my ride. I'll see you later, Mama."

"Have fun."

Zita called goodnight to her foster sisters who were in the living room watching television, grabbed her purse and headed outside. Rebecca's small green hatchback pulled up with a guy behind the wheel.

"Hi!" Zita said as she opened the door. "You must be Chad." He was probably mid-twenties, and dressed casually in jeans and a black hoodie that had seen better days. Not quite what she thought of as date attire, but maybe she'd got it wrong and this was supposed to be a casual night out.

"Yeah. Zita, right?"

She nodded, getting in and doing up her seat belt.

"I hear there's a steakhouse near here," he said.

"There sure is." Zita wasn't particularly keen on it, but Rebecca had said her cousin didn't do any kind of fancy food. As she gave him directions, she checked him out. His seat was pulled quite far forward, which meant he had to be shorter than her, maybe five foot five. His dark hair stuck out in different angles, but looked more like he'd forgotten to brush it than by design.

They pulled into the parking lot, and after finding a table, she asked, "What brings you to Houston?"

His eyes welled up. "Broken heart. Needed a change of scenery." His voice was gruff.

"I'm sorry." She relaxed. He wasn't looking for a relationship.

"It was nice to be needed," Chad said a little wistfully.

Zita's heart went out to him. "I'm sure it was."

"She didn't really love me." There was bitterness there.

Zita's first reaction was always to soothe, but today she didn't have the energy. Today she wished she could date someone who just wanted a good time, no strings attached. She chose to keep the conversation light. "What do you do?"

"I'm searching for work. No one is hiring at the moment. I wouldn't have thought finding a mechanical engineering job would be so difficult down here."

"Have you had much experience?"

"Some, here and there."

Though she knew she was going to regret suggesting it, she said, "My sister works at an oil refinery. I can ask if they're hiring at the moment."

"They probably aren't."

Could he be less enthusiastic? "It never hurts to ask."

"If you want."

Wow, he wasn't willing to put any effort in. "I'll contact you if there's something." She added it to her mental to-do list and picked up the menu. "Shall we order?" The quicker they ate, the faster she could escape.

Conversation drifted to what they were going to eat and then to movies they had watched recently.

"Jessica didn't like mainstream movies," Chad said. "She said they were trash wrapped up in a shiny package."

Zita resisted rolling her eyes. "And what do you think?"

He shrugged. "I like the blockbusters."

"Great. What's your favorite?"

She continued to prompt him for information, but it was like getting Carmen to stop prying. Almost impossible. Not once did he ask her anything about herself.

When her phone rang, she lunged for it. "I'm so sorry," she said to Chad. "I thought I had it on silent." Her finger brushed the answer button. She winced. "Hello?"

"Zita, it's David Randall."

The deep tone of his voice was enough to make her smile. "Hi, David. How are you?"

"Good. Do you have time to talk about the meeting today?"

She glanced across at Chad who was staring morosely at his beer bottle. "I'd love to, but I'm out at the moment."

"Oh, right." His disappointment was clear.

"How about I call you tomorrow night?"

"That would be great."

She hung up.

"Who was that? Rebecca said you didn't have a boyfriend."

She frowned. "It was work related."

"Why is he calling after hours then?"

She didn't have to explain, but he looked hurt. "It has to do with the charity I work for. David knew I was busy this afternoon."

"Right." He didn't ask her anything further.

A date with David would have been much better than this. He would have at least asked some questions.

At the end of the night, they went to pay for the meal. Chad didn't reach for his wallet.

"Shall we split the bill?" Zita asked, determined to remain friendly.

"Isn't your sister a billionaire?"

Zita took a step back. "Yes, she is. However, I am *not*."

"She doesn't give you any money?"

It was none of his damn business. "No," she lied. She was very aware that her car and her lifestyle were thanks to her sister, but she didn't take advantage of it. In fact, she would have preferred if she'd had to go out to earn money, then she could do what she wanted.

With a scowl, he opened his wallet and took out his share.

Zita was relieved to get into the car. It was almost over.

"Want to go back to Rebecca's place?" Chad asked.

Zita almost laughed. Had he been absent at their date? Was he so self-absorbed, he didn't realize how badly he'd crashed and burned? "No, thank you. I've had a long day."

"Rebecca said you liked a good time."

She was not going to ask what he meant. "What I'd like is to go home."

He grunted and drove her back to Casa Flanagan. The moment the car pulled up, she leapt out. "It was nice meeting you," she said. She slammed the door and hurried up the steps.

Why was it so hard to find a decent guy? She was good-looking and friendly. How come she always attracted the men who had issues or needed mothering? It couldn't be too much to ask for a well-adjusted, emotionally stable man who had a decent job and who could make her laugh, could it?

She opened the door and then locked it behind her. Chad had already driven off.

Perhaps she went on too many blind dates. Her friends always had someone to introduce her to, but they were one-night-stand worthy and not much else. Chad hadn't even been that. She definitely wasn't going to let Rebecca set her up any more.

Her thoughts drifted to David. He seemed stable enough and was definitely worth a second glance. Perhaps after they were done with Teresa's case she would ask him out to dinner. He couldn't possibly as bad as Chad.

No one could.

With a shake of her head, she headed for bed.

***

David walked into his apartment, relieved he was finished work for the day. He'd been thinking about Zita and Teresa since the session yesterday and had been unable to focus. He needed to ask Zita questions, express his views, talk through the commotion in his mind.

But she'd been out.

He'd been tempted to ask her if she'd been on a date, but it was none of his business. Their interaction was purely professional.

For now.

It would be great to take her out to dinner. She'd be an interesting conversationalist, he was sure. Her world view and experiences were far different from his. He knew a little about her childhood from Carly. She'd grown up poor, migrated to

Houston when she was young and now worked with the illegal child migrants who were arriving in the United States by the thousands.

He checked his fridge for something to make for dinner. There was a leftover curry from the takeout he'd had the night before, so he put it in the microwave and reheated it. As he sat down at his dining table, he opened the folder he'd put together with the information about Teresa's case. While he was sure Shelly and Zita were doing everything they could to help Teresa, David wanted to record the details and gather evidence on his own. He worked better if he wrote everything down.

He jumped as his phone rang. Then he saw the caller ID and smiled. "Zita."

"Hi, David. Do you have time to chat?"

"Yes." He pushed his meal away.

"Great. I'm sure you have a lot of questions."

"Did you have a good time last night?" He winced. He didn't know why that was the first question to come out of his mouth.

She laughed. "Worst blind date ever," she said. "I've forbidden my friend from ever setting me up again."

He relaxed. "My friends' wives are constantly trying to find me someone. Luckily my friends usually head them off. It's only when I have dinner at their place that I can't escape."

"At least then you've got someone else to talk to." She sighed. "I want to put the date far behind me, so what can I help you with?"

That's right. He needed to focus. "How's Teresa today?"

"She's as good as can be expected. She's more worried about her sister than she is about her own refugee application."

"What's the deal with that? Is her sister in danger?"

"We're not certain, but we suspect so. The gang will be angry Teresa escaped, so there's no telling what they'll do in retaliation." Zita sighed. "Fernando spoke with Johanna once, but there was no sign of Teresa's sister, Manuela."

"How old is she?"

"Twelve. I'm hoping it makes her too young to be prostituted out, but there's no guarantee."

David's jaw dropped. "Really?"

"Really." She sounded sad.

He thought that kind of stuff only happened in movies. He wanted to cheer her up, but how could he? This was her reality. "Do many of your foster sisters have similar stories?"

"Teresa's is the worst I've heard in a while."

He huffed out a breath. "Is Teresa the only one still waiting for her application to be processed?"

"No. We've got two other girls who are applying for Special Immigration Juvenile status. It would break my heart if they were deported." Her voice wavered.

"Will you tell me about them?"

She sighed. "Beatriz is ten. Her stepfather abused her physically and mentally and she decided she'd be better off alone. She found out Elena was leaving Guatemala and joined her. Elena had been raped by a gang and when she discovered she was pregnant, she knew they would force her to stay with them. She's due to give birth in a month."

David couldn't fathom what it would be like fleeing your country and having to deal with an unplanned and potentially unwanted pregnancy. "How did they get here?"

"They walked, hitchhiked, hopped the trains."

"Isn't that dangerous?"

"Yeah. They call the train The Beast, and so many are killed or severely injured trying to ride it. Then there are the people who monitor the trains and extort money from whoever's riding them."

"And if you've got no money?"

"You can be pushed off. The girls are often sexually assaulted as payment."

Coming to the States wasn't the easy option he'd thought it was.

"How will you get the rest of Teresa's family out of El Salvador?" he asked.

"They can submit an application for asylum, or if Teresa is accepted she can apply on their behalf. The problem is contacting them. Teresa's father usually answers the phone and we can't risk telling him. He's terrified of the gangs and doesn't want to do anything to upset them further. He's likely to try and stop us."

"And your contact, Fernando, can't help?"

"Johanna won't trust him, and Fernando can't risk visiting too frequently or the gang will get suspicious."

David couldn't imagine what it would be like to be scared of talking to someone. "Why is the gang issue so bad? Can't the government do something?"

"During the civil war, the violence was horrible, and people fled to the United States. They formed gangs here to protect themselves, and then in the nineties they were deported back to El Salvador because they were causing so much trouble. The gangs picked up from where they left off, terrorizing the local people."

He didn't know that. Who was he kidding? He knew nothing about the situation. His father's voice echoed in his ear. *'Don't believe everything you hear.'* He shut it out. Sure, he'd do his research later, but if Zita was lying, she deserved an award. It was tearing her up. "Is there some way I can help?"

"The biggest problem is that the issue can't be solved by letting in all the refugees. It has to be stopped in the country — reduce the divide between rich and poor, increase education, stop the corruption in the government and the control of the gangs. Some of the girls want to return home after they've got their degrees, but it's dangerous." She was silent a moment. "If you want to do something you could support Casa Flanagan, or educate people like your father."

"Dad listens to reason. I'm sure he got a lot out of the symposium." His father liked to bluster and get reactions from people, which gave them the wrong idea.

"If you say so," Zita said. "I've got to go. If you've got any more questions, just call. Do you want to come to Teresa's other meetings?"

"Yes, please. I'd like to keep up to date with what's happening with her family as well." Now he'd heard their story, he couldn't forget it.

"Of course." She sounded surprised. "I'll keep in touch." She hung up.

David suspected getting involved in the immigration issues was going to be more time consuming than he'd expected, but he couldn't help it. He couldn't in good conscience ignore what he'd learned.

He got to his feet to reheat his meal. He also wanted to see Zita again. She wasn't like the women he normally dated. She wasn't sophisticated, or fashion conscious, or worried about what people thought. She didn't appear to care who he was, or how much he was worth. She didn't seem interested in him in that way at all.

He smiled.

Hopefully he could change her mind.

***

David walked into the lounge bar on New Year's Eve and scanned the room for Carly and Evan. It was a gorgeous venue for their engagement party, and aside from the celebration, he was looking forward to seeing Zita again. It had been a few weeks since Teresa's meeting and he hadn't heard anything from her.

The first thing he noticed was that he was in the minority. Most of the room was full of Hispanic women, though there were a few men as well, and the conversation was largely in Spanish. It was the first time he'd ever been conscious of being a white male. It was a strange experience, slightly unsettling.

Then he saw the tall, strawberry blonde wearing a yellow evening dress that had ruffles like a flamenco dress down the split and showed a lot of leg, and he forgot all about being the odd one out.

Zita.

She went over to the bar to order herself a drink, the dress flouncing with her. His groin stirred. The way she moved, confident and completely unaware of her body, was pure seduction. He followed her.

"Hi, Zita."

She smiled at him. "David. Nice to see you."

"You look lovely tonight." That was the understatement of the evening. He brushed his lips over her cheek and was rewarded with a sharp intake of her breath. "How have you been?"

"Busy," she said. "Christmas is seriously crazy at Casa Flanagan. Almost all of our foster sisters come home and the house is overflowing with people."

His own Christmas had been at his parents' mansion with all his cousins, aunts and uncles. They were loud and raucous so he knew what she meant. "That must be nice."

Zita took her margarita from the barman and, not wanting her to leave yet, he asked, "Do you want to have a seat?" He gestured to the lounge chairs near them as he ordered a glass of red wine.

"Sure."

He picked up his glass and moved over to the seats, placing the present he'd brought on the table. He didn't want to talk about her work tonight. "So, were you on Santa's naughty or nice list this year?

She chuckled. "The jury's still out on that."

"Is that so? What did you do that was bad?"

She looked him up and down, her eyes assessing. "If you're lucky, you might find out."

David grinned. "I usually have great luck."

"I'm sure you do." She crossed her legs and the split in her skirt shifted, exposing her thigh in an almost indecent manner.

If she shifted a little bit more… he shut down that thought. This wasn't the place to get aroused.

"Oh, two of my sisters are at the bar." Zita sat up straight, watching them. "I need to check what they're ordering. They like to push the limits sometimes." She stood and smiled at him. "Hopefully I'll see you later." She walked off.

David watched her go, her hips swaying as she walked. He shifted in his seat. He definitely wanted to spend more time with her. He'd seen her fiery, and also empathetic — an unusual combination.

Across at the bar, Zita said something to her foster sisters, who must have been about sixteen. Their shoulders slumped and they were handed what looked like a cola drink.

He smiled.

Spotting Carly and Evan across the room, he set down his glass and wandered over.

"David!" Carly kissed both of his cheeks and gave him a hug. Evan shook his hand.

"Congratulations, Carly. I'm happy for you." Carly had grown from a very shy, uncertain teen, into a powerful and successful businesswoman. She'd been his confidante at too many gala events to count, keeping him sane, letting him make outrageous comments about some of the other attendees, which he daren't make to anyone else. "This is for you." Suddenly nervous, he handed her the small gift. Would she even remember?

"David, the invitation said no presents."

"Open it," he prompted.

She opened the box and stared at what was inside for a moment, her mouth dropping open. Then she burst out laughing. "You didn't!"

Relief flooded his body. She remembered.

"I'm guessing there's a story behind this," Evan said as he picked up the rose-colored glass bowl, which was supposed to be shaped like a flower, but looked disturbingly like a part of the female anatomy.

"I'd forgotten all about this," Carly said and turned to Evan. "It was one of my first gala events and the woman who was organizing it was relentless about asking all the guests for more money. We were supposed to leave donations in these bowls, but when it came time to do it, ours was missing. The organizer was most upset."

"Was the gala raising money for cervical cancer?"

David and Carly laughed.

"I believe it was literacy," David said.

Evan shook his head.

"What are you all laughing about?"

David turned to the small Hispanic lady who had joined the group. She looked very much like Carly.

"Mama, David was reminding me of one of my first gala events." Carly said, "David, this is my mother, Carmen."

"I saw you at the symposium. You're following Teresa's case, aren't you?" Carmen asked.

"Yes, ma'am."

"Are you learning much?"

He nodded. "A lot."

"Good. Excuse me, I believe Alejandra needs my help." She walked toward a teenager holding a baby.

Carly placed the lid back on the box. "Thank you. I'll cherish this," she said. "What's this about you following Teresa's case?"

"I met Zita at the symposium a few weeks back. I wanted to find out more about the refugee situation and she offered to help."

Carly looked troubled. "Teresa has been through so much."

Evan nodded. "She's so sweet, and a wonderful artist."

"She's not sure about me," David admitted. "Though that's not surprising, considering what she's been through."

"So why the sudden interest?" Carly asked. "We've known each other for years and you haven't asked about it."

He shrugged. "We never talked about your charity." Their conversations revolved around the galas they attended, or business. "The symposium was an eye-opener. Your speech was fantastic."

Carly glanced away. "Thank you."

"It must be so difficult for Zita to deal with the foster girls every day, and know what they've been through."

"Mama helps. They both support the girls."

He looked around the room. Zita was laughing with her sister Bridget. Her whole face lit up and she looked so happy and carefree. He definitely wanted to get to know her better. Evan cleared his throat and David turned back to them. They were both grinning at him.

"What?"

"Are you checking out my little sister, David?"

He cursed himself as the flush spread across his face. He hadn't blushed since he was a teenager. "She seems nice." Hell, this was awkward.

"You should ask her out," Carly said. "She needs to find a decent guy."

She wouldn't think he was decent if she could hear his thoughts. "Thanks. I'm going to say hello to Hayden."

He escaped before they could tease him anymore.

***

Zita was relieved to walk away from David and resume mingling. His simple kiss on her cheek had played havoc with her senses, and her body had kicked into high alert mode. He'd smelled divine — some kind of musky, masculine aftershave that made her want to keep sniffing him — and the brush of his lips against her skin made her want more. He was the type who had a different woman on his arm at each event, but she was fine with that. Right now she just wanted to have some fun.

At first she'd thought he'd wanted to ask more questions about Teresa's case, and was pleased when he didn't. Tonight she wanted to relax and celebrate. Tonight she wanted to pretend that bad things didn't happen to good people, and the world was a fair and just place.

Now it was almost midnight and everyone around her was watching the clock. On other New Year's Eves she'd be looking for a guy to kiss, but men were in short supply at this event. She hadn't even seen David for a while so perhaps he'd already gone home. Out of the corner of her eye, she saw someone moving toward her. She turned as the countdown began.

Ten.

Her eyes met David's and the intensity of his gaze stirred her.

Nine.

She couldn't look away.

Eight.

Her body zapped to attention as he strode toward her. His movements were long and languid, and sexy.

Seven.

The countdown faded into the background as she licked her lips.

David stopped in front of her, his gaze still on her.

"Happy New Year!" The shout went up around her, but she barely noticed it.

"Happy New Year, Zita," he said.

She didn't hesitate. She wrapped her arms around his neck and brought her lips to his.

Instant heat.

She'd meant to keep it light, but the moment their lips met, she sank into him, deepening the kiss. He tasted like wine and more. His hands slid over her waist to her lower back as he pulled her closer. Zita moaned in appreciation. This man could kiss.

Suddenly a wolf whistle split the air, piercing her

consciousness and she broke away. Around her people were watching and clapping.

"*Feck*," she muttered. She glanced up to a smug-looking David and said, "Happy New Year."

"I'll say," he said with a smile.

"Show's over, folks," she said and everyone returned to what they were doing. "Sorry. I got carried away." Now her brain was kicking back into gear she realized he'd probably only come over to wish her well and she'd forced herself on him. How embarrassing.

"I'm not." He took her hand and led her into the corner. "Want to get carried away again?" His wicked grin sent her hormones into overdrive.

"Yes." She stepped forward, but her mother's laugh from somewhere nearby was like a bucket of cold water being thrown over her. She stopped David with a hand on his chest as she searched the room and found her mother only a few feet away, keeping half an eye on them.

David followed her gaze. "Ah, your mother."

She nodded. "Let's take a rain check."

"How about dinner? Next Friday."

A little thrill spread through Zita. "Sure."

"I'll make a booking and give you a call with details." He glanced toward Carmen who was still watching them. "I should probably go."

She walked him to the exit. "I'll talk to you later." She brushed her lips against his one last time.

"Happy New Year." He walked out.

Zita let out a long breath. It certainly seemed like it was going to be a great new year.

<h1 style="text-align:center">Chapter 3</h1>

Everyone slept late on New Year's Day. Everyone, that is, except Julio, Alejandra's four-month-old baby, who started crying at about five in the morning. Zita woke and listened to Alejandra trying to quiet him. It wasn't working, and one of the other girls yelled in Spanish, "Take him downstairs."

There was likely to be an all-out argument if Alejandra didn't and Zita was too tired for that. With a groan, she got up and padded across the hallway to Alejandra's room. "Do you want me to take him?"

Alejandra was pacing the floor with Julio, looking stressed. The relief on her face was obvious. "He's been fed, but he won't settle. Tiana doesn't understand." She glared toward Tiana's bedroom.

Zita took the baby from her. "I'll see what I can do." She cooed to him and rocked him as she carried him downstairs, away from the bedrooms so the others could sleep.

In the living room, her dogs greeted her with wags of their tails, but didn't get up. It was too early for them as well. Zita settled herself on the sofa, Julio against her chest, and murmured nonsense to him. His cries grew softer.

She closed her eyes. She was so tired. After she'd gone to bed last night, she hadn't been able to stop replaying her kiss with David in her mind. She'd not been expecting the passion, the intensity and she couldn't wait to see him again. She smiled.

Julio hiccupped and stopped crying. Zita shifted him so he was next to the back rest and the two of them fell asleep.

The noise from the television being switched on woke them both. Zita sighed, opening her eyes as Julio started to cry again. Beatriz was fumbling with the remote to turn the volume down, glancing at her fearfully.

"I'm sorry. I didn't see you," Beatriz said.

"It's all right, Bea," Zita soothed, and sat up, shushing the baby. "What time is it?"

"Seven."

Last night, Beatriz had curled up on a sofa at the bar and fallen asleep way before midnight. "Did you have fun last night?"

Beatriz nodded and sat on the sofa next to Zita, making faces at Julio. He stopped crying and watched her in fascination.

"You're good with babies," Zita said, smiling at the girl.

She looked up. "There were many babies in my neighborhood. I helped with them to stay out of Pablo's way. The mothers appreciated my help."

"I'm sure they did."

"I promised Elena I'd help with her baby when it comes. I like babies. They don't hurt you." Beatriz held out her hands to take Julio and Zita passed him over.

Her heart went out to the ten-year-old girl.

Carmen ducked her head into the living room. "Already up, *niñitas?*"

"*Hola, Mamá.*" Zita stood and followed her mother into the kitchen. "Did you have a nice time last night?"

"It was wonderful," she said. "But I imagine you had more fun with David." Mama grinned at her.

Zita's cheeks heated. "I'm not answering that."

Her mother laughed. "He seems nice."

"I hope so." She didn't want to talk about it. She switched on the coffee machine, yawning.

"What time did Julio wake?" Carmen asked.

"Five."

"You should go back to bed, baby. You've barely had any sleep."

"I'm fine. I'll take the dogs for a walk and get some fresh air." She poured them both a coffee and sat down.

The first sip was heaven.

Just then, loud voices started yelling upstairs. *What now?* She glanced at Carmen, whose eyes were closed as if she was summoning the strength to deal with them. Zita got to her feet. "I'll check on them. You have your coffee."

"Thanks, *niñita*. I don't know what I'd do without you."

The words brought a stab of guilt. It was a reminder her mother couldn't do this on her own. She needed Zita's support. Any idea that Zita had about having her own life could be forgotten. With a small sigh, she headed upstairs.

By early afternoon, Zita was seriously considering running away. Surely a circus would have less excitement than Casa Flanagan. All of the girls had been tired and short-tempered. They'd snarked at each other and at Zita and Carmen all day. Carmen had spent hours calming a tearful Elena, who at eight months pregnant, had decided she didn't want the baby, which had left Zita playing referee to the rest. She needed some fresh air. She hadn't even had a chance to take Bess and Saint for a walk.

She shooed the girls out of the kitchen so she could clean up after lunch in peace. Hopefully, they would have an afternoon nap or hang out in their own rooms where they wouldn't argue.

Zita put the dishwasher on and was wiping the bench when Teresa came in. "Can we call Mama again, today?" She hugged herself, while looking hopefully at Zita.

How could she refuse?

Johanna might be in the kitchen cleaning up from lunch and be near the phone. "Let's do it now."

Teresa's grin was huge.

Zita dialed the number, thinking about what she would say if Johanna answered.

"*Hola.*" It was a female voice.

Zita tensed. "Johanna Garcia?"

"*Sí.*"

"My name is Zita Flanagan," she said in Spanish. "I'm taking care of your daughter, Teresa."

"Teresa," Johanna whispered. "Is she safe?"

"Yes. Can you talk for a moment? Is your husband around?"

"He is outside."

"I'll be quick then. Teresa is staying with us while her asylum application is being processed, but she would like to get you and Manuela out of the country as well. Would you like that?"

"Please." It was a sob that tore at Zita's heart.

"I have a friend in El Salvador, Fernando. He spoke to you a few weeks ago. You can trust him. He will tell you what you need to do. I'll get him to visit you next week."

"Thank you."

Their time was short. Teresa's father could come back at any stage. "I'll let you talk with Teresa."

She handed the phone to the girl and stood back while Teresa spoke with her mother. After a couple of minutes, Teresa hung up, sobbing and shaking.

Zita hugged her. "It's all right. We'll get them out."

Teresa shook her head and pushed her away. "No! It's not all right. The gang has taken Manuela. She's not yet been prostituted out, but Mama thinks it's only a matter of time." Tears rolled down her cheeks. "We *have* to get her out."

Zita wanted to throw up. Manuela was only twelve. "I'll call Fernando."

Carmen walked in from the garden. "What is wrong?"

Zita explained, and Carmen wrapped her arm around Teresa's shoulder and comforted her. Zita called Fernando, and he promised he would visit Johanna tomorrow. It was the best she could do for now.

Teresa had stopped crying and was staring at the table.

Zita wanted to scream. Life wasn't fair. This shouldn't be happening. They had done nothing wrong. Her heart pounded and her muscles were so tense they might snap. She had to get out of here before she exploded. She needed some air.

"I'm taking the dogs for a walk."

Carmen nodded and gave her a small smile.

Zita whistled for her dogs, got into her car and left.

***

Zita drove on auto-pilot to the state park. They had to get

Manuela and Johanna out of El Salvador as quickly as possible, but these things took time. The asylum application took months to process, and Zita wasn't sure they had that much time. She wanted to jump on a plane and fly them over herself, but they would likely be shipped right back home again and things would be far worse. Plus, she couldn't risk the criticism that would be directed at Casa Flanagan.

She swore. She wasn't as familiar with the asylum process as she was with the SIJ status that the girls normally applied for. She'd have to ask Shelly.

If she was an immigration lawyer, she'd know all the things they could try. Right now she was useless.

Pulling into the parking lot and stopping next to the only other vehicle in the lot, she turned off the car and got out. She should have brought boots. The ground was fairly muddy — the dogs were going to love it. Keeping them on the leash, she started down one of the walking tracks.

She breathed deeply, enjoying the coolness of the air and trying to relax. The bushes surrounding the wide path were heavy with the rain that had fallen earlier in the day and the air was still. Occasionally, a bird would call out or flit from bush to bush, shaking the drops from the branches.

Zita needed this. The peace, the time for herself. She needed it for her own emotional wellbeing.

She wasn't happy.

Her chest tightened at the admission, but it was time she faced the truth. She was twenty-five, still living at home, and couldn't see how she could possibly leave.

Guilt swamped her and she fought to stay on top of it. Was it so wrong to want to move out of home, to have her own space and her own things? She wanted to have a decent night's sleep, and be able to stay as long as she wanted in the shower, and to make herself toast for dinner if she didn't feel like cooking. But she couldn't leave her mother to cope with the girls on her own. It would be selfish and ungrateful. Her mother had left everything she had in El Salvador to give her daughters a better life.

Zita kicked a pebble on the path and it rolled a short distance before stopping.

That was her. Only getting so far before her momentum was lost.

As much as she loved her foster sisters, loved helping them and watching them grow, she wanted more out of life. She wanted an intellectual challenge as well as some level of independence. "I want to be an immigration lawyer." Saying the words aloud made her recoil with guilt, but it was true. She wanted to fight the battle for her sisters' freedom in the courtroom rather than staying silent in the crowd. She wanted to help more than the few girls who passed through their door.

But it meant going to college, then law school, and long hours of study. There'd be little time to help her mother care for the girls.

It was wishful thinking.

Bess barked at something on the path in front of them and Zita brought her attention to the present. It was a squirrel that quickly raced into the bushes.

Zita held both dogs back as they strained forward on the leash. It was foolish not to pay attention around here. There were poisonous snakes, and she'd spotted the occasional alligator as well.

Focusing back on the track she continued her walk. There was a place a little further on where she could sit for a while and contemplate.

When she arrived at the spot, she got the dogs some water and gave them both a treat, then sat down on the bench.

Perhaps it was simply the New Year blues. The whole "out with the old and in with the new". A time to set resolutions and plan for the future. But she didn't feel like she had the freedom to set her own goals.

She snorted, shaking her head at herself. She was being foolish. She had a hell of a lot more freedom than any of her foster sisters had ever had. She was rich in comparison. She lived in a beautiful house, in a country that respected her rights, and she had a supportive family.

And her family *was* supportive. If she was honest with herself, her mother would probably be the first to tell her to go to college.

So what was her *real* problem?

Sighing, she closed her eyes and sifted through her emotions. She was scared of failing.

In high school, she'd been a solid C-grade student. She'd been more interested in socializing than studying, until their first foster child had arrived, and after that she'd been busy helping Carmen. Her report cards had said she could do better if she applied herself, but was it true? Perhaps she wasn't cut out for study. Maybe she was too erratic to focus on one thing.

She certainly didn't have Carly's drive or technical skills, and even Bridget had channeled her passion into a career, but Zita had been keeping her own desires locked down for so many years, she wasn't sure she could unlock them now. Her mother had always told her she had to be strong for the girls, to hide her disgust or distress while they told their stories, and she had. She was so used to putting their needs before her own. And really, if she let her emotions out in the courtroom, she might be more of a liability than a help.

Her mind ran through all of the possible ways she could mess it up and cause one of her sisters to have to return home.

Bess nudged her foot as she shifted her position and the runaway train wreck of Zita's thoughts came to a halt. She wasn't usually this pessimistic. What if emotion was exactly what was needed? Perhaps being so close to her sisters would give her an edge to convince the judge they should stay in the country. She might be good at it, and she'd never shied away from hard work.

But she'd still have to find someone else to help her mother. Casa Flanagan might not be able to afford to hire a caregiver and she had no idea of the money involved. She only received a minimum wage. It was Carly who had the money.

She hunched into her jacket, pulling it close around her to ward off some of the chill that was setting in. She couldn't continue much longer like this. She would explode if she had to keep it bottled up inside. But it had to be little steps. She'd start by investigating law school and what was required.

Find out if she was smart enough.

Then she could work out what to do next.

Feeling a little more positive, she gathered her dogs, and started home.

***

David rang the doorbell at his parents' southern manor-style mansion and waited until the butler opened the door. He enjoyed dinner with his parents. It was a chance to see his mother, and the food was always sensational.

"Evening, Franklin." He walked inside.

"Good evening, Mr. Randall. They're in the sitting room."

"Thanks." He walked down the corridor into the large room. His mother was sitting on one of the large beige sofas that were as hard as they were stylish, talking with Jesse Harding's wife, Hillary. He frowned. No one had mentioned the Hardings were coming. David acknowledged the women and moved over to where his father and Jesse were talking at the fully stocked bar.

"David, there you are!" Bob slapped him on the back and handed him a bottle of beer from the fridge.

"Hey, Dad. Jesse. How are things?" He put the beer back into the fridge and poured himself a glass of white wine from the bottle the women were sharing.

"Jesse's still on at me to go into politics."

So that's why they were there.

"Your father is the perfect person — an upstanding citizen, successful, and knows how to run things. We need someone like him to take a firm hand."

David took a sip of wine. Bob had strong opinions, but his inability to compromise was legendary at Dionysus. It was all right in a business that had been in the family for generations, but in government? David wasn't so sure. His father was waiting for his response. "What about Dionysus?"

"You'd take over in an acting role until the election."

Damn. He thought he'd have at least another ten years before he'd have to step up. Suddenly his work life gaped below him like a bottomless pit. "I'm still getting my head around the CFO role."

"Now you don't have to," Jesse said. "If Bob agrees, you'll do a transition. He'll still be on hand to answer any questions."

David sighed. It was inevitable that he take over Dionysus, but he'd hoped it would be later rather than sooner. "You have my support, whatever you decide."

Bob nodded his thanks.

"We need to discuss what your policies will be," Jesse said. "Immigration is a big one. The flood of Mexicans needs to be stopped. We have to be strong on that."

"David here is following the process of the illegal immigrants," Bob said. "Making a case."

What? "I'm following Teresa's application so I have an idea of what is involved, but every person has a different story."

"Right, right," Bob said, clapping him on the shoulder. "We need to know more about it."

David let out a breath, pleased his father agreed with him.

Franklin walked into the room. "Dinner is about to be served."

David followed the others into the dining room.

Dinner was a three-course affair with Bob and Jesse dominating the conversation. David tried to picture Zita there and couldn't. There was no way she'd sit quietly while Bob and Jesse discussed politics. Her opposing opinion would make it an interesting evening.

He shouldn't be thinking about Zita meeting his parents. He didn't bring women home to meet his family and he wasn't even dating Zita yet.

At the end of the night, David said his goodbyes.

"We're still going to high tea on Sunday, aren't we?" Fay asked as she kissed him.

"Of course." It was their monthly ritual at the most expensive hotel in Houston. David would have preferred to meet in a café for coffee and cake, rather than having all the fiddly little desserts they served, but his mother insisted on the best. She was very conscious of what people thought of her, and David didn't want to disappoint her.

With a wave to the others, he got in his car and drove home.

***

Zita had been looking forward to tonight all week, and it wasn't just because she was getting away from Casa Flanagan. After parking her car, she checked her reflection in the rear view mirror. She hoped she was dressed fancy enough for the restaurant, but either way she felt great. She was going to dinner with the sexy David Randall.

Their sizzling kiss had been on her mind every night as she fell asleep. She'd thought about it so often that there was a real chance she'd blown it out of proportion, but tonight she'd discover if he did kiss as well as she remembered.

She got out and entered the restaurant. Everyone raved about The Wooden Spoon, but she'd never been there. Five-star restaurants weren't in her budget.

The spicy, warm aromas of delicious food hit her senses first, and Zita inhaled deeply as she glanced around. The furnishings were sumptuous. The carpet was thick and soft under her feet and the walls were an earthy tone, covered in artwork, much of it Native American. Everything was classy, from the crisp white tablecloths to the dim mood lighting.

David was sitting at a table by the wall, reading the menu. She studied him for a moment. He was wearing a deep blue, button-down shirt and the color suited him. His blond hair was styled in the messy, just-got-out-of-bed look that she suspected took an age to perfect, but suited him perfectly.

"Hi," she greeted him as she reached the table.

He grinned, pushed back his chair and stood. "You look fantastic."

The appreciation warmed through her, as did his kiss on her cheek. "Thanks. So do you."

He pulled out her chair and she sat. He had old school charm. It was a nice change.

As David sat back down, he asked, "Have you been here before?"

"No, but I've heard good things." The chef specialized in indigenous food. Zita couldn't wait to taste it.

They fell silent as they read the menu and when the waiter arrived they ordered.

"How was your week?" Zita asked.

"Fairly average. Lots of meetings." He smiled as he said it.

"What is it you do?"

"I'm the Chief Financial Officer at Dionysus Oil and Gas."

"Is that like an accountant?" She had no idea. Big business

wasn't her thing.

He laughed. "That's what I started out as. Now I oversee the whole financial side, but there are more politics and meetings to deal with than actual crunching numbers."

"Do you miss it — the crunching numbers?"

He was silent a moment. "Not at all."

Intrigued, Zita asked, "Why did you become an accountant then?"

"Dad wanted me to have a good understanding of financials for when I take over Dionysus."

"So you'll become CEO one day?"

"That's the plan." His smile didn't reach his eyes and he shifted in his seat.

"You don't sound excited about the prospect."

He shrugged, but didn't comment. Perhaps she shouldn't have mentioned it. "What do you do when you're not working?"

"I play golf, tennis, sometimes go sailing."

He probably belonged to a country club. Just the thought made Zita cringe. She imagined it full of people vying to outdo each other with how much they spent on plastic surgery or the latest car.

"Sometimes I go hiking with my friends," he added.

"There are some beautiful hiking areas around the city. I take my dogs there on the weekend."

"You have dogs?"

She smiled. "Yes. Bess is a lab-cross and Saint is a German shepherd. I rescued them from the pound a couple of years ago. I'd have more, but Mama's not as keen. They do tend to leave a lot of hair around." She wanted a whole pack of dogs. It had broken her heart to go to the pound and not be able to rescue them all. Though Bridget's partner Jack had been making noises about getting a dog soon. He and Bridget had moved into their new house and there was plenty of space, so maybe she could save another dog through them.

"I'd love a dog, but they don't allow them in my apartment building."

"Well, feel free to borrow mine any time you need a fix." The words were out before she considered them. She naturally shared what she had with others, but perhaps he'd think it odd, or maybe she wouldn't want to see him again. A sensational kiss didn't make a relationship.

"Thanks." He took a sip of his wine. "So what do you do in your spare time?"

"There's always stuff to do around Casa Flanagan — gardening, cleaning, helping Alejandra with her baby." Did it sound as pathetic to him as it did to her?

He shook his head. "That's work. What do you do when you go home?"

She hesitated. It was always awkward when she had this conversation with guys. "I live at Casa Flanagan. That is my home. I help Mama with the foster girls." She waited for the usual reaction.

He frowned. "You live with your mother?"

There it was. "Sure do." She kept her voice light. "Taking care of six girls is a lot of work, and we also help the migrant community."

David was silent a moment. "So do you get time off?"

"I get a few hours on the weekends. I take the dogs and explore the different hiking tracks around Houston."

"I bet they love that."

She grinned. "They sure do."

Their food arrived and it smelled amazing. Zita took a mouthful, and the flavors burst on her tongue. "This is delicious."

David nodded in agreement. "The chef is so good."

She cast her mind around for something else to ask. "Have you considered moving so you can get a dog?"

"No. Too much hassle."

He obviously wasn't that keen then.

David took a sip of his wine. "I hear Evan's exhibition did really well last month."

She grinned. "It did. I'm so happy for him. I wish I was as talented."

"You paint?"

"Not really. The most creative I get is sewing."

"That's something. I can't tell one end of a needle from the other."

"One end will prick you." She laughed.

"Yeah, OK, I knew that." He smiled.

Damn. The way his eyes crinkled at the sides and the hint of the dimple in his cheek sent her senses into overdrive.

"Do you sew very often?"

She pushed the lust down. "When I have time." Silence fell and she added, "I had to learn to sew. When we were younger, Mama couldn't afford a lot, so I had to alter Bridget's hand-me-downs."

"That must have been rough. You migrated to the States when you were young, right?"

She nodded. "I was three. I don't remember much about El Salvador. My first memories are living in a tiny little apartment, sharing a room with Bridget, and Mama working at a nursery. She didn't earn a lot, but we managed."

"Was it hard for you to learn English?"

"Not at all. My father apparently used to speak English to all us girls, and when we moved here, Carly taught me until I went to school. It was pretty easy after that."

"Being bilingual must be handy."

"Sure." The conversation paused as they ordered dessert. "Do you speak any other languages?"

"I know a little bit of a lot of languages," David admitted. "Enough to say please, thank you, where is the bathroom, that kind of thing."

He liked to be polite. It said a whole lot about him. "Where have you traveled?"

"I travel a bit for work — Australia, Canada, Europe. My favorite place is probably New York. It's so busy and energetic."

That sounded awful. Her life was hectic enough as it was. "You like to be busy?"

"I like people, and the vibe that everyone has somewhere to be, something to do."

She understood to a certain extent. There were times when she loved the vibe of Casa Flanagan, but if she ever got away for an extended period of time she wanted to do nothing but sit on a beach and read a book.

As the dessert was served, David asked, "So you have six foster sisters?"

"Yes, plus baby Julio. Larissa and Tiana are the oldest at

sixteen, and Alejandra is fifteen. She's Julio's mother."

"That's young to have a baby."

She nodded. "The girls who get involved with gang members often get pregnant. They don't use contraceptives. Alejandra wanted more for her baby than life in a *mara* so she came here."

"Was she a member?"

"Yeah. She didn't like what they did, but there was little choice."

"I'm surprised the government let her in. I thought they were cracking down on gang members."

Zita's annoyance flared and she tampered it. "It's not like that. Where she was living it was safest to align herself with a *mara*. But then a rival gang came in and killed a bunch of members and she realized her baby was at risk. If she stayed he'd be inducted, and she didn't want that. The life expectancy for a gang member in El Salvador is about thirty-five."

His eyes widened. "Seriously?"

"Yeah. The situation is that bad. Can you understand why Alejandra left?"

He nodded. "I would have too."

Zita relaxed. He understood. There were some people who refused to put themselves in the refugee's shoes, refused to contemplate what it was like in these countries, and that made it almost impossible to help them understand why so many were fleeing to the United States. David's empathy made him all the more attractive.

"Would you like to order coffee?" The waiter was back to collect their dessert plates.

"We could have coffee at my place." David's smile sent tingles through her.

She suspected it was a euphemism, but she was fine with that. She'd like to get him alone. "That sounds like fun."

David turned to the waiter. "We'll have the check, please."

Chapter 4

David unlocked his apartment door and held it open for Zita to enter. Flicking on the light, he pulled Zita toward him and brushed her hair behind her ear. "I've had a nice evening so far."

Her smile seemed a little mischievious. "Me too."

Lowering his head, he brushed his lips against hers, gauging her reaction. She murmured her approval and he drew her closer, needing more of her. He deepened the kiss, tasting her, and she slid her tongue over his lips. He grew hard. She was so hot.

Zita broke the kiss and put a hand on his chest. "How about that coffee?"

It took a second for her words to register. She wanted coffee?

She moved down the hallway to the kitchen and sat at his breakfast bar. David took a second to regroup. This wasn't how things normally went, but he could run with it. "How do you take it?"

"Cream, two sugars please." Her smile was sinful.

Perhaps she didn't like to rush.

He switched on the coffee machine. Should he put some music on as well? No, that would be too cheesy. As he poured milk into his milk frother, his hand trembled. Women didn't normally get him this worked up, but Zita was addictive. One kiss from her left him aroused in a way he'd not experienced before.

She was different.

He was selective about the women he brought home. He made sure they understood he wasn't after a relationship. But it was more with Zita. She wasn't just sexy, she was also interesting to talk with. He'd had a meaningful conversation with her each time they spoke.

He handed Zita her coffee.

"Thanks." She spun on her stool so she was facing the living room. "That's a great photo." She pointed to the canvas on his wall. "It looks like the bayou."

He wandered around and sat next to her. "It is. I took it a couple of years ago."

She turned to him. "Really? It's fantastic."

"Thanks." He was particularly proud of it.

"Do you like photography?"

He liked the admiration on her face and wished he could say he was good at something, but the truth was he wasn't. Why was Zita's opinion of him suddenly so important? "It was a lucky shot," he admitted. "I took it on my phone." He sipped his coffee.

"The photos I take on my phone always look like they've been taken by a two year old; I've got my finger in the picture, or it's off-center or wonky."

He laughed. "As I said, it was luck."

She grinned and placed her mug on the bench behind her. She picked up a book, and too late he realized it was the latest fantasy he was reading. His coolness factor was plummeting by the second.

"You read fantasy?" she asked, turning the book over to read the back.

"Sometimes." He shrugged.

"I love it. It's my favorite genre." Zita put the book back down.

"Really?" The last woman who'd discovered he liked fantasy had called him a nerd.

"Absolutely. I love the magic, dragons and epic quests."

"Favorite author?"

"Ugh, too hard to decide. What about you?"

"Tolkien has to be up there," David said.

Zita screwed up her face. "He's a bit wordy for me."

David gaped at her. "Wordy?"

"Yeah. All that Gloin, son of Thoin, son of Foin stuff. It's too hard to remember."

He shook his head. The detail was the best bit. "What series do you like then?"

"Pretty much anything with dragons."

Perhaps this was something that would impress her. "Anything up there?" He pointed to his bookcase.

She got to her feet and wandered over to browse. "Oh my God, check out this collection!"

He grinned. She looked so cute, standing there with her head tilted so she could read the spines.

"I'd marry you for this alone." Her words were light, but they hit a tender spot in his heart he'd not realized he had.

He glanced down at his mug. He'd thought tonight was about sex, but the pain from her words suggested that maybe it wasn't. He enjoyed talking with her and had already been thinking about their next date. He was used to women wanting him for his money, but he *had* thought Zita was different. Though he never would have picked his book collection as a selling point.

"Hey, are you all right?" Zita hurried over, laying a hand lightly on his arm.

"Of course." He forced a smile.

"I was kidding about the marriage comment," she said. "I'm not in the market for a husband."

"You'd be the first." He didn't know where the words came from or why he was so upset. He knew he was a 'catch' and had always used it to his advantage.

Zita frowned. "Yeah, well, I'm a bit busy at the moment for a relationship."

Darn it. He had to snap out of it. She'd been joking. He had this gorgeous woman in his house and she liked the same kind of books that he did. That was a win.

"Perhaps I should go," she said.

"That's probably a good idea." The words were out before

he could stop them. What was wrong with him?

She nodded, her face showing her concern. "Of course. I'm sorry." She got to her feet, grabbed her purse from the table and headed to the door.

He followed. "Zita . . ." What could he say? Part of him was screaming at him to pick up the ball he'd dropped, but a different part of him, one he hadn't really heard before, was telling him not to bother. "I'm a little tired."

"It's fine. It's late." She turned back to him, a cautious smile on her face. "I had a nice time tonight." She leaned in and pressed her lips against his.

They were warm and the kiss was sweet, but it wasn't enough to shut off the voices in his head.

She stepped back.

He opened the door. "Drive safely."

She pressed the button on the elevator. "I'll call you when we get Teresa's court date."

He nodded, wishing he could say something else. Wishing it was just sex he wanted from her.

He froze.

The elevator arrived with a ding and she got in. As the doors shut, his body relaxed, but his heart thudded loudly in his chest. He rested his forehead against the door frame.

For the first time in his life, he wanted more from a woman.

And he didn't like the sensation at all.

***

Last night was a mess in Zita's head. She'd had a lovely time at the restaurant and she smiled, remembering the surprise on David's face when she'd asked for coffee. He'd been so cocky and sure of himself, and she'd wanted to slow things down, make him not take her for granted. But then she'd made one silly flippant remark and ruined it all. The disappointment on his face and the way he'd shut down made it clear his wealth was an issue for him. She'd been careless, not considering her words, but it had also surprised her.

During dinner, she'd slotted David into the fun-to-hang-out-with category, but their backgrounds were too different for anything more. She'd recognized his line for what it was, and thought it would be a fun way to end the evening, but then he'd honestly been upset by her comment.

And she'd missed out on the sex.

With a groan, she got out of bed and threw on a track suit. She'd not slept well and wouldn't be going back to sleep now. Jogging down the stairs, she called to her dogs and headed to the kitchen. She didn't have time to take them on a long walk today, but hopefully throwing the ball in the garden would be enough to help her clear her head. She grabbed an apple and the dogs' ball and headed out the back to the large grassed area at the rear of the property.

Zita threw the ball and both dogs raced after it. When Bess returned it, she threw it again.

She'd hurt David, and she wasn't entirely sure how to make it up to him. Apologizing again would help, but they were just words. She hated to make anyone feel bad.

Sighing, she threw the next ball with more force. She should decide whether she wanted to date him again. He intrigued her more now he'd shown a sensitive side, but she'd been honest the night before when she'd said she wasn't after a husband. Right now she didn't have the extra emotional capacity for a relationship, even if she wanted one. She was busy with the girls and if she explored her options to become a lawyer, she'd have even less time.

Still, that kiss at Carly's engagement party was up there on her top three. That had to count in his favor. She wouldn't mind kissing him again, and more. But he may no longer be interested.

She checked the time. David would probably be up by now. She'd call, say sorry and go from there. She dialed his number.

"Hi Zita." He sounded surprised.

Perhaps she shouldn't have called so soon. Maybe he'd think she was really interested. "I wanted to apologize again for the thing I said last night," she said. "It was careless of me."

He sighed. "I know you were joking. It hit a raw spot, is all."

"Yeah, well Carly has the same one, so I should have known better. I've been worrying about it all night."

"You needn't have. I was kicking myself for suggesting you go. We could have had a great discussion about which fantasy series has the best dragons in it." His tone was playful.

She grinned, relieved he was fine, but still wishing she could see his face to make sure. "Well, that's obvious, isn't it?"

"Oh really?"

"*The Emperor's Conspiracy.*"

"Not in a million years," he replied and promptly told her all the reasons she was wrong.

After debating the issue for quite some time, Zita laughed. "I'd better go. The battery on my phone is almost dead and I don't want to hang up on you."

"Where are you?"

"The dogs and I are at the back of Mama's property." Both dogs had tired of fetching the ball and were sleeping under a tree.

"Have you got any plans later? We could go to the movies tonight, if you want."

"I can't." She was surprised at her level of disappointment. This was the real David and he was fun to talk with. "We're having a girls' night at Carly's tonight."

"How about Sunday?"

"I need to take Teresa to art class in the morning. How about in the afternoon?"

"Darn, I forgot that's my afternoon with Mom. How about next Saturday?"

"Sure. Why don't we talk during the week and sort something out?" Her battery was in the red now.

"OK."

Zita hung up feeling a lot better. If the conversation was any indication, David wasn't upset about her joke. He was available for some fun, and she could definitely find some spare energy for that.

Grinning, she called to her dogs and headed into the house.

***

Nausea rolled in Zita's stomach as she rode the elevator up to Carly's penthouse apartment that night. It was silly. All they were doing was going over the few old photos they had from their time in El Salvador and talking about their father.

A couple of months ago, during the Day of the Dead

celebrations, she'd discovered her father hadn't died in an accident at work like she'd thought. He'd been murdered while helping someone in their village. She'd been upset to learn the truth, and in her state she'd blurted out the secret she'd kept her whole life.

She didn't remember her father.

It was ironic, since she was the only one who'd taken after him in appearance. Carly and Bridget both resembled their mother, with dark curly hair and darker skin, though Bridget had inherited their father's height as well.

Zita supposed she should be pleased she had something to remember him by, that she only had to look in the mirror, but it was difficult. She knew nothing about her Irish roots and her appearance meant she didn't physically fit in with the Hispanic community. She'd spent years dressing traditionally for any events, in order to feel like she was part of them.

The elevator doors opened and she knocked on Carly's door. Bridget opened it with a glass of wine in her hand. "You're late."

"Traffic," Zita explained, kissing her sister's cheek and walking in.

She hadn't been here since Evan had moved in and she smiled at the easels set up in front of the floor-to-ceiling windows in the living room.

"Dinner's arrived," Carly said, motioning to the boxes of Chinese food on the dining table.

"Great." She was starving. She took a seat and grabbed the nearest container. "Where's Evan?"

"He and Jack went to the movies," Carly said.

"I know we're here to talk about Papa," Bridget said as she dished up some food. "But first, I want to hear about your date with David."

"I'm not sure I want to," Carly joked, putting her fingers in her ears.

Zita smiled at her sisters. "Not much to tell. We had dinner, he showed me his book collection and I went home."

"He took his book collection to the restaurant?" Bridget asked.

"No, I went back to his place." Her face heated. She

regretted that she usually told her sisters all the details of her dates.

Bridget raised an eyebrow. "That bad, huh?"

"No! I mean, it was fine — nice. Nothing happened." *Feck.*

Carly studied her and Zita offered her the carton of food to distract her. "Where did you go to dinner?"

"The Wooden Spoon." She stuffed some food in her mouth.

"Holy hell! That's like the best restaurant in Houston," Bridget said. "Someone was out to impress."

"Or just has a lot of money," Zita countered, annoyed.

"True. Does he have a trust fund?" Bridget asked.

"I don't know!" Zita glared at her sister. "And I don't care. I'm not dating him for his money."

"But you are seeing him," Carly said.

"Yes. No. It was one date." Her sisters didn't normally rile her this much.

"Got another one planned?" Bridget asked.

"No." It wasn't a lie. They hadn't planned what they were going to do next Saturday.

"I always thought he was nice," Carly said.

"Then you should have dated him," Zita fired back.

Carly laughed. "Ew. That would be like dating my brother."

The fire in her stomach tapered. "You never fancied him?"

"No. Never." Carly squinted at her. "And he never fancied me."

It was a relief, though she'd never admit it aloud. The thought of David with Carly was just ick. "So, how are the wedding plans coming along?"

"Not quite as slowly as the house plans. Hayden and Mama are having fun."

Hayden was Carly's PA and had started putting together wedding information for Carly, without being asked to. When Carmen had found out, they'd formed a wedding planning team. Carly barely had to do anything.

"What about you?" she asked Bridget. "Any plans yet?" Bridget and Jack had bought a house together, but weren't engaged.

Her sister smiled. "I was thinking about proposing to him next weekend."

Zita's mouth dropped open. "That's fantastic!" She was so thrilled both her sisters had found the men they wanted to spend the rest of their lives with. She jumped up and hugged her sister.

"Yeah, I'm fairly sure he'll say yes."

Jack had been enamored with Bridget since they'd first met, but it had taken her some time to trust him. He'd agreed to take their relationship at the pace Bridget needed.

"Mama's going to be thrilled," Carly said.

She would be. Two daughters getting married was going to flip her mother out. Zita cleared the empty boxes from the table and then took her sisters' plates. She wasn't sure why she was feeling a little sad.

"You ready to go through the photo album?" Carly asked her.

Zita let out a breath. Was she? "I guess so."

Bridget gave her a hug. "It's not so bad, ZZ. We all have issues about Papa dying so young."

Zita looked at her sister. "Really?"

"Sure. One of the reasons I got into workplace safety was because I thought Papa had died at work. I didn't want anyone else to go through that." She glanced at Carly.

Carly sighed. "And I felt like I had to take care of you all, because I'd promised Papa I would."

Perhaps Zita wasn't the odd one out after all. She walked over to the sofa and sat down, her sisters sitting either side of her. Carly handed her the photo album. The first few pages were of Carly, Bridget and their parents before she was born. Her mother was so young, younger than Carly was now, and she looked so happy. There were photos of the four of them together, smiling. Her father had a look on his face as if he couldn't believe how lucky he was. The love shone out of his blue eyes.

He was lanky and far taller than Carmen, but that wasn't difficult, considering Carmen was just under five feet. He was probably about Bridget's height, and his hair was the exact color of Zita's, though it was short and disheveled in most of the pictures.

As she flicked through the photos, her sisters told her stories of where they were taken and what had been happening at the time. It was Carly who spoke the most. She was the eldest, five years older than Zita, and therefore recalled a lot more, but there were a few things Bridget remembered.

"This was taken the day you were born," Carly said, pointing at the photo where Zita first appeared. It was a family photo, her mother looking a little tired, her father pleased as punch, and Bridget awkwardly holding Zita with Carly helping her. "Papa said he had his three princesses."

"Did he ever want a boy?" Zita asked.

"Mama once said they would have liked a boy as well," Carly said.

They continued through the photos until they reached the end. It didn't take long as there were so few. It would have been lovely to have photos from when her father was a child.

"Have you ever searched for Papa's family?" Zita asked.

"No," Carly answered. "Mama always said his parents were dead and he had no siblings. It was one of the reasons he was happy to stay in El Salvador." She glanced at Bridget. "Have you?"

Bridget shook her head. "I figured any relatives we did have in Ireland would only be distantly related and wouldn't care about us."

Zita was silent. Her Irish family had always fascinated her, but she'd never been brave enough to search. She was worried she might upset her mother, make her think that she wasn't good enough, but it wasn't that. It was the tenuous idea that she might have people who looked like her, and who could tell her more stories about her father. But there was no guarantee they would welcome her into the family, and that was the main reason she'd never gone further. Still, looking at these photos made her want to know more. Surely he would have an aunt or an uncle who remembered him?

"I'd kind of like to," she admitted. "Find out if they have anything of Papa's. Do you think Mama would mind?"

Carly shook her head. "No. Do you want a hand?"

"No. I'll do a search when I have a little bit of time."

"All right," Carly said, getting to her feet. "There's one more thing. I found it when I was going through the box of things

Mama kept from El Salvador, and got it digitized." She switched on her laptop that was sitting on the coffee table. She smiled at them both. "Neither of you have seen it." She clicked on a file and a movie came up.

A home movie.

Zita gasped.

"How have we never seen this?" Bridget asked, as shocked as Zita was.

"I asked Mama and she said she didn't have anything to play it on and had forgotten about it."

The movie was of their parents' wedding, her mother looking beautiful in a white dress with matching bolero and her father in a blue suit. They were in a little church that was packed with people.

"That's the church in our village," Carly said.

It was strange to watch a walking, talking version of her father. All of a sudden, he was alive again. Zita listened as they said their vows, her father in halting Spanish with the most horrendous accent. She giggled. "Papa sounds awful."

Carly laughed. "He must have learned quickly. I remember him speaking it fluently, though still with an accent."

The video changed to show the family farm and the house where they had lived with their grandparents, and then went through each one of the girls' christenings. Carly must have edited them together. Zita's heart swelled as her father held her and kissed her forehead so tenderly. It was obvious he loved her. Tears pricked her eyes.

"This is my favorite bit," Carly said as the setting changed again to the beach.

It had to be the day at the beach that Carly had spoken about at the last Day of the Dead celebration. The three of them were building sandcastles, their father next to them, patiently helping and giving them encouragement. Carmen called from behind the camera, "Time to wash up."

Her father jumped to his feet. "Last one in is a rotten egg," he said and raced for the water. Carly was on her feet in a flash, racing after him and after a moment's stumble, Bridget was after her. Zita, however, was the slowest. She got to her feet and ran as fast as her little legs could carry her. Carly and Bridget were already in the water, shrieking and splashing, but her father was encouraging her, jogging slowly so she could catch him.

"Beat you, Papa," Zita called as she got to the water and then she tripped and fell into the waves. Her father scooped her out, wet and bedraggled and gave her a huge hug and a kiss. "You sure did, *a leanbh*."

Tears streamed down Zita's face. Her father had loved her. He had held her, and kissed her, and waited for her. She took the tissue Bridget handed her and the three of them wiped their eyes.

"Has Mama seen this?" Bridget asked.

"Not yet," Carly said.

"We'll need to buy a carton of tissues before she does," Zita said, sniffing. She hugged Carly. "Thank you."

"You're most welcome, *niñita*. Now you can see how much Papa loved us all."

She could. She really could.

Chapter 5

David checked his reflection in the mirror for the third time. Jeans, long-sleeved red top, and his long black cashmere coat. He nodded in approval. He wanted to make a good impression on Zita after he'd spoiled their last date.

He'd overreacted to Zita's comment – got way ahead of himself. It was just because they hadn't jumped straight into bed after arriving at his apartment that he'd mistakenly thought he wanted more. It was ridiculous. He was too young to settle down.

He checked that he had his phone, wallet and keys, and then headed down to the foyer to wait for Zita. She'd insisted on picking him up, stating it was easier for her to come to him as she lived on the outskirts of Houston. She'd also told him she'd arrange the details of their second date, so David had no idea what they were doing. He wasn't used to being the one waiting and in the dark.

Zita pulled up in the unloading zone outside his building, so he hurried outside.

"Hi, how was your week?" Zita asked, flashing him a grin as he got in the car.

He smiled back. "Same as always." She looked great in a bright red fifties-style dress and white tights. "Lots of meetings and people wanting to increase their budgets."

"Is it your job to say no?"

"Yes. My eye has to be firmly on the bottom line, but there are some projects that would be worth spending money on." If only he could convince his father.

"That must be hard. I'd be hopeless at it. I always want to please people."

He nodded. "Yeah, I'm not the most popular person at work." But he didn't want to talk about it. He needed to make up for their last date. "Where are we going?"

She grinned at him. "Discovery Green. There's a flea market on today."

He raised an eyebrow. Was she kidding? He hadn't been to a flea market since he was in college and his friends had dragged him to one. He glanced out at the dark clouds threatening rain.

"There are a whole heap of food vendors there and I thought it might be fun to try something different."

"Sounds good," he lied. The last thing he wanted to do was pretend to be interested while someone tried to sell him a second-hand toaster that had seen better days.

Zita managed to find parking immediately. The market was set up in a shady area of the park and the stalls were a myriad of color, displaying their wares. It wasn't too crowded and as David got out of the car he smelled smoky barbecue and some other spicy scent. His stomach rumbled. If it tasted as good as it smelled, it might not be too bad.

"Let's eat first." Zita shrugged into a long lime-green coat and then grabbed his hand and led him over to the food vendors. They walked side by side, and Zita didn't seem to notice she was still holding his hand, but he did. Her hand fit comfortably in his. There was no awkwardness. Strange that he'd never paid any attention to holding someone's hand before.

They walked along the trailers of food. The Brazilian barbecue was responsible for the delicious scents. "How about here?"

"Great idea." Zita pulled out her wallet. "I'll pay."

David tensed. "No, I will." He'd been taught a gentleman paid for a lady.

"Don't be silly. You paid last time." She handed over some money as he reached for his wallet.

He withdrew some bills and held them out to her.

She shook her head. "Put it away." She held her hands behind her back and gave him a don't-mess-with-me stare.

He replaced the money. "I'll get dessert."

"Sure." She smiled.

Pleased she agreed with him, he took the meal he was handed and they moved onto the grass under some trees and sat down.

"This smells so good," Zita said and took a bite of her spicy meat. "Mmm," she hummed, swallowing. "Tastes good too."

He swallowed as well, as her blatant enjoyment stirred something inside of him. He shifted his position and took a bite of his own meal. It *was* good.

"Played any golf this week?" Zita asked.

"No, it's been too dark by the time I finish."

"Of course. Do you work crazy hours like Carly used to?"

"I try not to. If there's nothing urgent, I leave around five. I don't tend to take work home, but lately there have been a few extra reporting requirements."

"So what do you do after work?"

"I've been catching up with my reading and overdosing on comic book TV series." He waited for her reaction.

"Ooh, what are you reading?" She leaned forward, grinning.

He loved her enthusiasm, and the fact she read fantasy novels as well made him feel far less of a geek. "The latest Jane Dargatz."

"I haven't read that series yet, but I've heard it's good. What do you think?"

"I love it," he said and went on to explain why. By the time he was done, they'd both finished eating.

"I'll have to add the series to my to-be-read list," Zita said, scrunching up the packaging. "Do you want to wander around the stalls?"

"Sure." He'd pretend to be interested.

Reaching the first stall, he let out a soft exclamation of surprise. Home-made jewelry — earrings, bracelets and necklaces — all professionally worked. The next stall had leatherwork and the next, second-hand furniture that had been lovingly restored. This flea market was letting craftspeople show their wares. It was a celebration of creativity, not a junk yard.

Zita went from stall to stall, chatting with the owners, praising the quality of the work and asking at the recycle stalls what she could do to help the environment. She was so in the moment and encouraging. He could tell each owner felt good talking to her. That was an incredible talent.

Along the way she also bought things: a bottle of lotion from one stall for Alejandra, a scarf from another for Beatriz. "Mama will love this," she said, holding up a beaded necklace. "How much?"

After she'd paid for the jewelry, David asked, "Have you bought anything for yourself?"

She smiled at him. "I don't need anything." She moved on.

She was fascinating. Whenever he went shopping with his mother and sister, they bought so much — clothes, makeup, jewelry — all for themselves, even though their wardrobes were already overflowing. Was that the difference between growing up rich and growing up poor? You understood the value of an item more when you couldn't have it.

The next stall had a collection of metal pieces — fob watches, necklaces, all very steam punk. Zita picked up a watch, and ran her thumb over the intricate links in the chain.

"This is beautiful," she said to the owner.

"Thank you."

She put it down again with a sigh.

"Do you like it?" David asked.

"I love it," Zita admitted.

"So why don't you buy it?" He was curious. She had no problem buying things for everyone else.

"I don't need it. It's just a fancy." She turned to walk away.

He placed a hand on her arm. "Does your mother need the necklace you bought?"

"Well, no." She bit her lip.

"So why did you buy it?"

"Because she'll love it."

"Like you love that watch?"

She looked longingly at it. "Yes."

He took it off the table and handed it to the stall owner. "I'll take this, please."

Zita gasped. "No. Don't be silly, David."

He ignored her as he paid and took the package. "For you," he said, holding it out to Zita.

She put her hands behind her back. "No. I didn't expect you to buy it for me."

"I know." There was no artifice with her. She wasn't the type to say one thing and mean another. "It's a gift."

"David, it's sweet, but I can't accept it."

"Sure you can. I've already bought it and it won't suit me." He smiled at her, guessing what would convince her. "You don't want me to have wasted my money, do you?"

She squirmed. "No."

It fascinated him that she was so reluctant. She was so generous to everyone else.

"I wasn't giving you a hint."

His stupid reaction from the other night was working its way into their date. "I *know* that, Zita. Take the bag."

She took it and peered inside. "Thank you, David." She stepped closer and brushed her lips against his cheek.

He resisted the urge to turn his head so her lips met his. It wasn't why he'd bought it. "You're most welcome."

Zita took the watch out. "Will you help me put it on?"

He took it from her, undid the fiddly little clasp, and placed it on her slim wrist before doing it up again.

She ran a finger over the clock face. "It's gorgeous."

It was also inexpensive. He didn't understand why she hadn't bought it herself.

They walked on, stopping at a stall to buy treats for Zita's dogs, and then at a stall run by a Hispanic woman who was maybe a couple of years younger than Zita.

"Daniella," Zita greeted the young woman. "How's business?"

"It's a bit slow today. The weather keeps people away."

"It's not that cold," Zita said. "Daniella, this is David." She turned to him. "Daniella is one of my foster sisters. She lives in one of the little cabins out the back of Casa Flanagan."

"Nice to meet you," he said, shaking her hand. The stall contained beautiful ceramic items. "Did you make these?"

Daniella nodded. "It's a hobby of mine."

"Daniella is studying political science," Zita told him. "She hopes to one day go back to Honduras and make a difference."

It took a lot of bravery to go back to a country she'd fled from. "That's admirable."

Daniella shook her head. "I want to stop other girls from going through what I did."

He didn't ask what that was. He didn't want to pry. Instead, he looked at the bowls and chose a medium-sized one. "I've wanted a fruit bowl," he said, handing over the money.

Daniella wrapped the bowl in tissue paper and placed it in a paper bag. "I hope you enjoy it."

Zita and Daniella chatted for a little longer and then said goodbye.

As they wandered to the next stall, Zita said, "You didn't need to buy the bowl."

"I did need a bowl and hers are lovely."

She squinted at him as if to see whether he was telling the truth.

He smiled at her. "Honest." Why was she questioning his motives? They walked past a pie van. "Want some pie?"

"Sure."

He bought them both a slice and they carried it over to a nearby seat. "Do you come here regularly?"

"It's only on once a month, and I like to stop by to check how Daniella is doing. It can get a little boring being in a stall by yourself."

"Don't the other stall owners speak with each other?"

"Yeah, they do, but they're all busy at different times."

"How long have you known Daniella?"

"Nine years. She was one of the first foster girls we had," Zita said. "She was only a couple of years younger than me and yet she'd been through such horrific things. I realized then how lucky I was that Mama got us out of El Salvador."

"How old were you?"

"Sixteen."

It must have been a hell of a thing to realize. At sixteen, he was focused on study and girls, not necessarily in that order. His only worry was getting good enough grades to get into college. But Zita had been shown a world where things weren't so simple.

"Did you ever resent the foster girls?" It had to have been difficult if all the girls had been abused.

"Would it make me a bad person if I said I did?" Her voice was quiet.

"No, it would make you human."

She sighed. "There were times when I was having a bad day, or needed help of my own that I resented not having Mama's full attention. Both Carly and Bridget had moved out before the first foster girl arrived, so they didn't know what it was like. I mean, how could I complain about a friend being nasty, or a boy not asking me to a dance, when these girls had been abused, had lived in poverty, and had undertaken the dangerous journey to the States by themselves?" She was so matter-of-fact, but there was sadness in her tone as well.

David wrapped an arm around her shoulder and pulled her closer to him. "Your life experience was different from theirs. You had the safety and security to be able to worry about things they may have considered inconsequential. But it doesn't mean that a friend being mean to you didn't have an impact in your world."

"Knowing that didn't make it a whole lot easier."

He wasn't sure what else to say. He would have hated anything that disturbed his perfect world.

Big, fat raindrops started to slowly fall. "It's about to rain."

She looked around. "Where's the nearest shelter?"

Others had already gathered under the stall shelters. "There are denser trees over there," he said, pointing. "They might give us better cover."

The rain was coming faster now.

She grabbed his hand. "Let's go."

Together, they ran across the grass as the drops got thicker. By the time they reached the shelter of the trees, water was dripping from his hair. His coat was heavy and the occasional drip ran down his top. He dropped her hand and squeezed the water out of his hair.

Zita laughed, carefree and delighted. "We got a bit wet."

He stared at her. Why was she laughing? "I think you're right." The bottoms of his jeans were also soaked and uncomfortable.

Zita took off her bright green coat and shook it. Drops flicked off, but there was no significant change in its dampness. She glanced out at the downpour, then turned to him, a mischievous grin on her face. "Have you ever danced in the rain?"

Was she kidding? It was cold, and the moment they stepped out from under the canopy they would get completely drenched. "No."

She placed her bags at the base of the tree, took off her new watch and put her coat back on. "Want to?" she asked, holding out her hand, her expression gleeful.

She was serious. They were wet and she wanted to get soaked.

Zita beckoned to him playfully.

He couldn't refuse, not when she was that damn appealing. He put his hand in hers and let himself be pulled out into the rain.

He'd been right. He was drenched in seconds. Zita twirled around, arms outstretched, face up to the sky and laughing in delight. His heart twinged, and suddenly he didn't care about the rain. She was incredible.

He snagged her hand and pulled her close to him. "May I have this dance?"

"Absolutely, my kind sir."

They did a rough impression of a waltz, the rain beating down on them and water slipping down his shirt. He laughed with Zita and embraced the moment.

Finally, the rain stopped and they stopped twirling, both breathing heavily.

"It's *fecking* freezing," Zita said, hugging herself.

She was right. The water had seeped into his clothes, down to his underpants and socks. Ugh. "I've got hot coffee and dry clothes at my house."

"Let's go." She dashed back to the tree to grab her purchases and then they hurried to where she'd parked her car. Zita put her bags in the trunk and grabbed two clean dry towels. She tossed him one. "This might help."

"Why do you have towels in your car?"

"They're for the dogs. They often get mucky on our walks."

After drying himself the best he could, he got into the front seat. Zita started the car and turned on the heating. Now he was still, the cold was setting in fast. His hands were like ice.

"Damned traffic," Zita said as they hit a traffic jam. She shivered. "Whose idea was it to dance in the rain?" she grumbled.

He laughed, his teeth chattering a bit. "I believe that was you."

"Well, next time, tell me I'm an idiot."

"Never. That's the first time I've ever danced in the rain and I don't regret a second." It was incredibly freeing.

"Really?"

"It was fun," he said.

"No, I meant, was that really your first time dancing in the rain?"

He nodded. "Not something we ever did when we were kids."

"Why not?"

He shrugged. "It never occurred to me."

She glanced at him quickly and then back at the road. He couldn't decipher her look.

As a child, he'd always been conscious of who was around. He represented the Randall family wherever he went and he always behaved.

He'd not considered that a bad thing until now.

Chapter 6

By the time they arrived at David's apartment, the car's heating had kicked in, but his clothes were lying wet and uncomfortable against his skin. "Do you want a hot shower?" he asked Zita. "I can loan you some dry clothes to put on."

"That would be great."

He switched on the wood-fire-look gas heater and hurried into his bedroom to get some clothes for her. Sweatpants, sweater and T-shirt should be fine. He then grabbed a clean towel and showed her into the guest bathroom.

"Do you want to have the first shower?" she asked.

"I've got another bathroom. I'll take a shower there."

"All right." She shut the door.

He tried not to think about her getting naked as he hurried back into the living room. The apartment was still freezing and his movements were stiff as he set up a drying rack in front of the fire and hung her coat over it. By the time he was finished, he was shivering. He showered in record time, not daring to spend too long under the luxuriously hot water, in case Zita was waiting for him when he got out.

He'd given Zita his favorite comfort clothes, so he threw on a pair of black sweats and a green woolen sweater he'd bought on his last skiing trip. When he hurried back to the living room, it was empty. A glance out of the window showed the rain had settled in for the day.

"I feel so much better." Zita's voice had him turning around.

She was adorable in his slightly too big clothes and her hair wrapped up in a towel like a turban.

"Do you have a clothes dryer?" she asked. "I squeezed out my clothes, but it might take them a while to dry."

He wasn't in any rush for her to go, but he said, "Sure. It's this way."

They threw their clothes in together, her underwear landing on top of the pile. He froze. She was going commando. His body stirred at the instant visual his imagination conjured. Clearing his throat, he set the dryer going and accompanied her back to the living room.

"Take a seat by the fire," he invited. "Do you want a coffee, or hot chocolate with marshmallows?"

"Ooh, hot chocolate please."

She curled up on the sofa. He appreciated her ability to make herself comfortable wherever she went. She looked like she belonged there. He headed for the kitchen and a few minutes later he returned, handing Zita her drink.

"Thanks." She took the mug and blew on the top, before taking a careful sip. "Delicious."

"Are you warm enough?" He sat next to her, relaxing into the soft cushions.

"Just toasty," she said. "Thanks for lending me some clothes."

"My pleasure. Thank you for showing me the joys of dancing in the rain."

"Any time." She grinned.

Her smile warmed him, making him want more of her. But he was comfortable, relaxed, there was plenty of time for sex later. He'd never sat on a couch wearing dorky clothes and drinking hot chocolate with a woman. It was kind of nice.

"So what else have you never done that you wished you had?" Zita asked.

For a second, he thought she'd read his mind, but then realized she was referring to dancing in the rain. He raised his eyebrows. "I don't know." He had the funds to do most things, but saying it aloud would make him sound spoiled. "What about you?"

"I'd like to be able to drop everything and fly somewhere for the weekend — Vegas or Hawaii or Cancun."

"You've never been to any of those places?" he asked.

"No. I haven't been far from Houston since I arrived. When we were kids there was never the money, and now, I can't leave Mama alone with all the foster girls. It's too much work. There's always someone needing help."

He frowned. "What about you?"

"What do you mean?"

"When was your last vacation?"

"Carly once paid for us all to go to Lake Conroe for the week. There were about twenty of us."

"But that was with your family. When did you go away with friends, or by yourself?" He loved his family, but he didn't want to travel everywhere with them.

"I never have."

"Never?" He couldn't believe it.

She set her empty mug on the coffee table and crossed her arms. "No. Mama needs me."

"Do Bridget or Carly ever help?" She shouldn't have to do it all.

"They have real jobs."

He scowled. "But you have a real job."

***

The familiar frustration welled up inside Zita and she shifted in her seat. "It's not a job, it's just something I do. I've done a couple of counseling courses, and I follow Mama's lead."

"Don't you think what you do is valuable?"

"All I do is listen to the girls, help them with their homework, and talk to them in English so they pick it up quickly. It's not hard."

"Some people would find it difficult to listen to their stories, considering what those girls have gone through," David argued. "I know I did."

"You get used to it."

"You shouldn't have to." He reached over and put his arm around her, pulling her closer to him.

She leaned into him, breathing in his musky scent.

"So what would you do, if you had a choice?" he asked.

No one had ever asked her that. She peered up at him, surprised. His blue eyes looked into hers, no judgment there. His hand was running down her arm, soothing her, warming her. She hadn't expected this compassion from him. She sat up. "You mean if Mama didn't need me?"

He nodded.

"I'd go to college," she said in a rush, the thrill of admitting it quite terrifying.

"What would you study?"

"Law. I want to be an immigration lawyer." Her heart beat rapidly as she waited for his reaction.

"So why don't you?"

"I couldn't take that much time away from Mama and the girls."

"Have you spoken to Carmen about it?"

"Not yet."

"Why not?"

"Because she'd tell me to do it. But she'd struggle on her own." And Zita's fear of failure was real, like a gaping pit at the tip of her toes. She wasn't quite ready to confess her dreams to her family yet.

"Could she get other help?"

"It's not that simple. The girls are too sensitive at the moment. They would have to trust someone new, and I already know all the details of their cases. They need me." It was a good excuse.

"I'm sure something could be done. You're allowed to have your own life."

He was genuinely concerned for her and she didn't want to mislead him. Taking a deep breath, she told him the truth. "I wasn't great at school," she admitted. "Plus the hours are too much and it's expensive."

"Wouldn't Carly help pay?"

She frowned. "I can't keep running to Carly every time I need money. It's not fair on her."

"She's a billionaire, Zita. She's got the cash."

He didn't get it. "So I'm to be even more reliant on her than I already am? I don't think so." She shook her head. Her chest ached. Both her sisters were so successful. If she failed, she'd be the loser of her family. She couldn't bear the pity. She shifted in her seat. Enough talking about herself. She wanted to learn about him. "What about you? The other day you didn't sound all that enthusiastic about taking over Dionysus."

"It's always been assumed that I would."

She smiled. "Do you want to?"

He was silent a moment. "I'm proud of the company my family has built."

"That's not what I asked."

He ran a hand through his hair. "Hell, I don't know what I'd do if I wasn't working at Dionysus."

"There must be plenty of accounting jobs out there."

He grimaced. "I never really enjoyed crunching numbers."

"I can understand that," Zita said. "So what do you enjoy?"

He shrugged. "I helped my friend Garth set up his business and worked on a strategic plan for Colin. That was fun."

She knew very little about that kind of thing. "Could you make that into a business – setting up companies and helping them improve?"

"Probably, but it's too late now."

"Why?"

"Dad's considering going into politics."

"How will that affect you?"

"I've got to take over as CEO. There's always been a Randall in charge at Dionysus."

She frowned. "Do you have any siblings who would like to take over?"

He shook his head. "Grant's happy in maintenance and Lorelei has never been interested in the business."

"But that doesn't mean you should forgo what you want to do. It's your life, not your father's."

He raised an eyebrow. "Like you're standing up to your mother to become a lawyer?"

"Touché." It was far easier to help others than herself.

He stretched his arm over the backrest. "Will you talk to Carly? Ask if the charity can afford to hire another caregiver?"

Zita tensed. "It's fine. I've made a New Year's resolution to do something. So I've got all year."

"What are your target dates?"

"What?"

"There's no point having goals without setting targets and a date of completion. So what steps are you taking to reach your goal?"

She shifted further away from him, resisting the urge to get up and pace. It was easy to say she was going to do it this year — she still had three hundred and fifty days — but if she set specific dates it would become all too real.

"Zita?"

"I don't know." She clenched her hands.

He ran a hand over her arm. "I don't mean to push you. I'd like to help if I can."

She breathed out, trying to calm her heart rate. He was right. If she was serious about her dreams, she needed to make them happen. Needed to ignore her fear.

No matter how difficult it was.

Zita turned to him. "Where should I start?"

***

Together, they brainstormed her plan of action until Zita had specific steps to complete to become a lawyer. It was scary having it all written down with dates next to each step, though part of her felt lighter.

"You've got until the end of the month to talk to Carly and research admission to college," David said, handing her the plan.

She winced. "All right."

"That gives you two weeks to work up the nerve." He grinned at her.

She laughed. She couldn't help it. He looked so cheeky. "So what about you?"

"Me?"

"Are you going to talk to Bob about not taking over Dionysus?"

He hesitated. "I don't know. Dad wouldn't understand."

"How about your mom?"

He shook his head. "Let me think about it some more." David got to his feet and grabbed their empty mugs from the table. "Do you want another drink?"

"No thanks." She'd bring up the subject another time. He'd helped her, and she wanted to repay the favor.

David disappeared into the kitchen. He looked good. Zita had never considered sweat pants sexy, but he pulled it off. The pants were slung low on his hips, and his woolen sweater clung to his torso. She wanted to run her hands under his clothes and feel just how firm his chest was.

He returned with a packet of chips, which he offered her. "So, now you've decided to make this huge change in your life, what should we tackle next?"

She envisioned herself tackling him on to the sofa and straddling him. She forced herself to focus. "That's enough for now," she said with a smile. She checked her phone for the time — already four o'clock. She should probably head home to check if anyone needed help. But she was having fun hanging out with David.

"Do you have plans?" he asked.

She glanced up. "No. I was just thinking maybe I should check in to see if Mama's all right."

"Would she call you if she wasn't?"

"Probably not." Her mother was very self-sufficient.

"Then why don't you call her?"

"All right." She dialed her mother's number. "*Hola, Mamá.*"

"Zita. Is everything all right?"

"Of course. Do you need me home to help with dinner? Do the girls have any homework they need help with?"

"No, everything is fine. Are you having a nice time with David?"

"Yes."

"Then don't worry about anything. Will you be home tonight? The weather is awful for driving."

She cringed. There had been no suggestion from David about staying the night. "I don't know. Probably."

"Well text me if you're not going to be, so I don't worry."

"All right, Mama. I'll talk to you later." She ended the call. "All quiet on the western front?" David asked.

"Yeah. She doesn't need me tonight."

"Great. Do you want to stay and watch a movie? We could

order takeout. It's too wet to go out to eat, don't you think?"

He wanted to spend more time with her. Her body tingled. She was incredibly snuggly in the clothes that smelled like him, and the dryer was probably still running. "You're right. Takeout sounds great. What do you want to watch?"

"I've got cable."

"Then we should be set for the night." Her stomach wiggled in anticipation. Perhaps she shouldn't have said that. She could hardly invite herself to stay.

He flicked on his huge flat-screen television, pressed a few buttons and handed her the remote. "Do you want to choose something?"

"Sure. Got a preference?"

"As long as it's not horror, I'm good. Shall we order dinner before we start? There's a nearby Thai restaurant, or pizza, or Chinese."

"I don't care. Whatever you like."

"You're my guest," David smiled. "You choose."

Zita hesitated. She didn't want to get it wrong. "How about pizza? I haven't had that for a while."

"Great. Any preference on toppings?"

"I eat anything."

David ordered food while she flicked through the movie options. When he returned, she said, "We could go old school and watch *Labyrinth* or *Dark Crystal,* or we could go modern and watch *The Hobbit* or *Lord of the Rings.*"

"*Labyrinth,*" he said with a grin. "I haven't seen it in years."

She flicked through the menu and pressed play.

***

This was the most casual date Zita had ever been on. It was nice, relaxed, almost like hanging out with one of her friends. David flashed her a smile before concentrating back on the movie.

Almost. None of her friends' smiles made her body tingle. She wanted to take things further. Explore this man's body. Being cocooned in his clothes all afternoon had left her wanting more.

As the credits rolled, David turned to her. "That was great."

She nodded. "It's one of my favorite movies."

He switched off the television. "What shall we do now?"

She knew exactly what she wanted to do, but was he interested? There was only one way to find out. She shuffled a little closer to him. "We could make out on the sofa."

His eyes widened and his grin shot heat straight to her core. She leaned forward and kissed him.

His lips were firm. She deepened the kiss, wanting to taste him, and his arms came around her, one hand cradling the back of her head as they kissed. There was an intensity that sang to her. She climbed on to his lap, straddling him, wanting to get closer, to have better access.

David groaned as he ran his hands over her back. Her body was hot and she broke the kiss only long enough to shed her sweater and T-shirt.

Air flowed over her breasts and her nipples puckered. She'd forgotten she wasn't wearing a bra. Oh well.

"Jesus, Zita," David groaned and caressed her breasts. "You're so beautiful." He pulled her closer so he could kiss her breasts and her head fell back as sensations zipped through her body. He was damn good with his tongue.

His erection was hard against her crotch. She wanted to see him. "You're overdressed," she murmured in his ear, her hands sneaking under his sweater.

"You're right." He shed his shirt and his bare chest pressed against hers. He was so warm, so luscious. She trailed kisses down his neck, her body throbbing more with each of his caresses. It was time for some more fun. She stood up, reached for her purse on the coffee table and slipped out the emergency condom she'd put there, before losing her sweat pants. David's eyes widened and he quickly took off his pants as well.

She straddled him again, kissing him firmly. "You ready for this?" She ground her crotch against his length.

"Hell, yes."

Zita grinned, and took hold of him, running her hand against his smooth, hard erection. He closed his eyes, his head back. "You're killing me."

She was killing herself as well. She wanted him inside her. Ripping open the condom packet, she sheathed him and then slowly lowered herself onto him. She closed her eyes. This was better. This is what she needed. She moved, setting a rhythm as he squeezed her bottom, moving with it. This was what she loved about sex — the closeness, the flow and the gorgeous build of tension before the release.

She rode him, pleasing herself as she pleased him. The sensations rose until she couldn't stand it any longer. She threw back her head, and together they came.

***

David's senses were slow to return to him. His body was hot, relaxed, and feeling oh, so fine. He hadn't been expecting sex. Not that he was complaining, no way at all. It had been incredible.

Zita kissed him slowly and then slid off, collapsing on the couch next to him. She was amazing, so sensual and not the least bit self-conscious about her body or what they'd done. He stirred again, and he got to his feet to clean up and slip on his pants. When he returned to the couch, she was still lying there, naked. She sat up to give him room to sit and he did, not quite sure what to say.

"That was fun," she said, kissing him again. "What do you want to do now?"

He was at a loss for words as she parroted what he'd said earlier. What did he want to do? He wanted to get her into his bed and explore her body, spend the rest of the night with her. He pulled her onto his lap, cradling her, and kissed her again. Thunder cracked and he glanced out the window at the rain continuing to fall. "It's awful out there. Do you want to stay the night?" He nuzzled her neck, wanting to be close. He didn't often invite women to stay, but he wasn't ready for her to go.

"Sure. Let me text Mama."

A glow went through him.

After she'd sent the message, he said, "I've got a television in my bedroom," he said. "Why don't we head in there?"

"Which way?" she asked, holding out her hand.

She walked hand in hand with him, naked, to his bedroom. She stopped at the entrance. "*Feck*, your bed is huge." With a whoop, she ran and jumped onto it.

He laughed at her exuberance. He'd never jumped on his bed, but it looked like fun. "Look out," he called and leaped after her. He landed with a soft thud and Zita grabbed a pillow, swatting him with it. He couldn't let it pass. Reaching for the other pillow, he was distracted by the way her breasts jiggled as she bounced on the bed. Instead, he pulled her on top of him and kissed her.

She grinned at him and murmured, "Something tells me we're not going to be watching any television." She slid her hand under his waistband and rubbed his already erect penis.

David closed his eyes. "I think you're right." He flipped their positions so he was on top. "But it's my turn to be in charge."

***

Zita stretched as she awoke the next morning, enjoying the pull on her muscles and the glorious limpness of her body after a night of great sex. Opening her eyes, she saw the bed next to her was empty. She hadn't felt David get up. She walked naked out of the bedroom and grabbed the sweater and pants she'd discarded the night before in the living room. She dressed, before moving toward the noises coming from the kitchen. David was wearing his sweatpants, frying eggs and bacon on the stove.

"Morning," she said.

He glanced over and grinned. "Morning. I hope I didn't wake you with all my racket. I wanted to make you breakfast in bed."

Her heart swelled. No guy had ever made her breakfast in bed. "No, you weren't noisy. What time is it anyway?" She kissed him.

"Ten."

She never slept that late. "It's Sunday, isn't it?" She ran a hand through her hair, thinking.

"Yes."

Damn it. "I'm supposed to be helping Mama prepare lunch. Carly and Bridget will be there soon." For the first time she really didn't want to go to the family lunch. She wanted a break from her commitments. David had proven to be more than a cute rich guy and she wanted to spend more time getting to know him. But it wasn't possible.

He frowned. "Sorry, I didn't realize you had plans."

"It's a regular thing. Every second week is family lunch. I completely forgot." It was not surprising, considering his shirtless state was distracting her again. Zita took a deep breath to calm herself. It was all right. One of the girls would help, she was sure, and she could see David another time. But she would need to head back if she was going to beat her sisters.

David dished up two plates of bacon and eggs. "Sit down and eat something. I'll fetch your clothes." He bent over and kissed her and her worries seemed insignificant.

"All right."

A couple of minutes later, he returned, handing Zita her folded clothes. "They're dry."

"Thank you." Now she'd eaten something and was more alert, she asked, "Have you got any plans for the day?"

"Nothing so far. I might go sailing."

"That sounds like fun." She wasn't ready for their date to end. She'd enjoyed herself yesterday and had been looking forward to spending more time with him today. But what would the girls say if she invited him to a family lunch? She wasn't ready for their inquisition yet. She wanted to keep this new, fresh and shiny relationship to herself for a while. If she exposed Casa Flanagan to him in all its glory, it might scare him off. She finished her breakfast and stood up. "Can I have a shower?"

"Of course."

She kissed him. "I won't be long." She had the quickest shower on record and dressed in her clothes from yesterday. When she came out, David was cleaning up the kitchen. "I'm sorry to eat and run."

"Don't worry about it. I should have woken you earlier."

"You didn't know." Her sisters were definitely going to beat her home. "Thanks for a great day yesterday."

"It was fun." He walked her to the door. "I'll call you later. Maybe we can do something next weekend?"

"I'd like that." A lot. She enjoyed being with him. It was so easy. She was able to talk to him about things that really mattered to her and he listened. It was a new experience for her.

She kissed him again slowly. "I'll see you later."

As Zita walked to the elevator, she smiled. Maybe she did have time for a relationship after all.

Chapter 7

Zita groaned as she pulled up at her mother's house to see Carly and Bridget's cars already there. She was bound to get some teasing. Bess and Saint started barking and ran to the car to greet her, foiling her hope to sneak inside and get changed without anyone noticing. She should train them not to do that.

After greeting her two lovable mutts, she let herself into the house and was met by a living room full of people. OK, so no hiding.

"Hey ZZ, did you run to the shop?" Carly asked, kissing her cheek.

"Ah, no."

"What do you call it in America?" Alejandra asked. "The walk of shame?"

The girls laughed as Zita's face heated up. "Nothing shameful about it," she said and then muttered to Alejandra, "Your English is too good."

Alejandra beamed at her and joined in the laughter.

"Who'd you go out with?" Bridget asked.

"I took David to the flea market," she answered, edging toward the staircase.

"Did you get lost?" Jack asked with a grin.

"Enough," Carmen said. "The weather was too dreadful to drive home, right *niñita*?" She winked at her youngest daughter.

Zita sighed. "Yes, Mama. Excuse me, I'm going to get

changed."

There was more laughter as she hurried upstairs.

***

When she returned, her mother called them into the dining room for lunch. The topic of today's discussion was Carly and Evan's wedding.

"Yesterday we went to check out the venue Hayden found," Carly said. "It's perfect for what we need."

"What's it like?" Zita asked.

"It has a room for the ceremony, kind of like a chapel, with big glass windows that look out on to the garden." Carly smiled. "It will be almost as good as being outside, without the heat."

"The reception room is large enough for dinner and dancing," Carmen said. "We can have a meal and celebrate with our friends."

"Have you picked a date?" Bridget asked.

"We were thinking July. Evan's parents will have vacation time by then."

"Then perhaps the end of August will be a good time for us," Bridget said, taking hold of Jack's hand. "Mama, can Jack and I get married in your garden?"

"Of course," Carmen said, and then she froze, mouth open as the words sunk in.

Bridget waved her left hand at her mother, showing the ring. "We're engaged!"

Carmen's shriek was enough to deafen them all. Zita grinned as her mother started crying.

"Congratulations," Zita said to Jack as she stood and hugged him.

"Thanks. I knew I'd wear her down eventually."

She smiled and kissed Bridget. "Congratulations, Birdy."

"Thanks, ZZ."

She moved out of the way so the others could congratulate the couple. It was wonderful to see her two sisters so happy. They deserved it.

Thinking about happiness reminded her she was supposed to talk to Carly about getting help at Casa Flanagan. Her stomach clenched, but now was as good a time as any. She moved over to her oldest sister. "Carly, can I have a private word with you later?" she asked. "We could maybe go for a walk in the garden."

"Sure." Her sister looked surprised.

They settled back at the table to discuss the two weddings. There was so much to talk about. Zita wasn't sure she could be bothered with all the fuss, but Bridget and Carly were excited about it.

After they finished eating they moved into the living room.

"I'll go pick the girls some vegetables to take home," Zita told her mother.

"Let me help," Carly said and together they went outside. Carly sighed. "I love this place. Mama's garden is always so gorgeous."

Zita couldn't see it the way her sisters did, couldn't appreciate the lush plantings, the plump vegetables hanging from the plants and the beautiful shade trees. All she noticed were jobs to be done: paths to be swept, branches to be pruned and fruit and vegetables to be picked before they rotted.

She walked to the broccoli and cauliflower bed and began to harvest.

"What did you want to talk to me about?" Carly asked.

Zita's stomach was in knots. How would her sister react? Was she being selfish?

"ZZ, what's wrong?"

She let out a sigh. "It's about Casa Flanagan."

When she didn't say anything else, Carly said, "Go on."

She braced herself. "Can the charity afford to hire another caregiver?" There, she'd said it, though she didn't dare look at her sister.

"Is there too much work for you and Mama?"

Zita shook her head. She had to be honest. Just get it all out. She took a deep breath. "I've been thinking of going to college."

"Really?" The surprise in Carly's voice was clear and Zita cringed. "What do you want to study?"

Perhaps she was a foolish dreamer. Perhaps she wasn't cut out for college. Zita put the vegetable heads in the basket and picked out a few weeds. "Immigration law."

Carly placed a hand on Zita's arm, and said, "Look at me,

ZZ."

She raised her eyes. Her sister was frowning.

"How long have you wanted to do immigration law?"

Zita swallowed. "For a few years now."

"*Why* didn't you say something?"

"Because Mama needs me. She can't do it by herself. She needs someone to take the girls to their meetings and teach the girls at home. She can't be in two places at once and the girls need someone they can trust."

"Of course we can find someone to help Mama. I thought this is what you wanted to do."

"I did . . . I do. It's just that I believe I could help them better in the courtroom."

"I'll talk to Mama about it. I'm sure she'll know someone in the refugee community who is able to help."

"No!" At Carly's surprise, she added, "Don't tell Mama yet. I need to find out more about the law degree. I might not qualify. There's no point getting her upset over nothing."

"Why would she be upset?"

"Because I've helped her from the beginning. She may think I'm abandoning her."

Carly raised an eyebrow. "You'll be learning more about the system, and helping the girls in court. That hardly counts as abandonment."

"She always says she'll be lost without me," Zita said quietly.

"It's an expression, Z. She appreciates your help, I'm sure she does, but if you're not happy, we have to fix it."

Tears rose to her eyes and she blinked rapidly to prevent them from falling.

"*Chiquita,* I'm sorry," said Carly. "I should have asked you what you wanted. We all assumed you were happy."

Zita didn't blame Carly at all. She'd always spoken up about small things she was unhappy with, but this was too big. It affected her whole family.

"Is there anything else you're not happy about?" Carly asked.

Zita glanced around the garden. Was it best to fix one thing at a time? Would she appear like the most ungrateful cow if she asked for more?

"What is it, Z?" Carly urged, her voice stern.

Her throat choked up. "It doesn't matter."

"Of course it does."

She shook her head. "I'm being too selfish."

"You're the most unselfish person I know, Zita Flanagan, so spill."

Zita sighed. "Eventually, if we find a caregiver, I'd like to move out of home. I'd like my own space."

"Oh, *niñita*. Of course you can. We've been so neglectful of you, making these assumptions while you've been unhappy all this time." Carly pulled her into a hug.

"Not always. Just lately."

"We're going to fix it. You find out about law school and tell me what the next step is."

"All right."

"We should go in, otherwise Mama will wonder what we're up to," Carly said, getting to her feet.

"You're right." Zita didn't need her mother asking questions.

***

Zita woke early on Monday morning before the girls were up.

She fed Bess and Saint, who were always quick to appear when anyone was in the kitchen. Alejandra came in, carrying Julio.

"I didn't hear him last night," Zita commented. "Did he sleep through?"

"Yes. He was a good boy." Alejandra took a seat at the breakfast bar while she breastfed her son.

Zita placed a bowl of cereal in front of her.

"Thanks, Zita."

The other girls came downstairs one by one, dressed for the day. Elena was getting slower and slower, with her pregnancy causing her a lot of discomfort. She was due any day.

Carmen came inside from the garden and fussed around Elena. "We've got a doctor's appointment tomorrow."

Elena widened her eyes and shook her head quickly. "No. I am fine. The baby will come when it is ready."

Zita saw the girl's fear. There was a high infant and maternal mortality rate in Guatemala, where Elena had lived and often the 'doctors' in the poorer areas didn't have the proper qualifications.

Carmen clucked her tongue, but didn't say anything else.

Zita checked the time. "The bus will be here soon." Her words brought on a flurry of activity as Alejandra kissed her son and handed him to Zita, and the other girls gathered their things together. In a very short time, they were out the door.

It was quiet for a moment, until Julio started crying. With a sigh, Zita carried him out into the garden to give the others some peace. He was always upset when Alejandra left, and a walk around the garden usually settled him, but today Zita was tired. After her sisters had left yesterday, she'd been busy helping the girls with last-minute homework. By the time it was done, she was too tired to investigate law school as she'd planned.

But she would do it today. Her mother would take the girls through their English lessons in the morning and she would be able to sit down in peace with her computer.

"Zita, come quickly!" Her mother's call was urgent.

Zita hurried down the path to the house and rushed inside. "What's wrong?"

"Elena's waters just broke." Carmen had a mop in her hand and was cleaning up the mess.

"Any contractions?"

"No."

"Ahhh," Elena screamed.

"Yes," her mother amended.

At Elena's scream, Julio started crying again. Beatriz and Teresa were standing to the side, wide-eyed, and Beatriz looked frightened.

"Teresa, take Julio and Bea into the living room," Zita said, giving Teresa the baby. "I'll be in shortly." She turned to her mother. "I'll grab her bag from upstairs."

Carmen nodded, holding onto Elena's hand.

Zita rushed up the stairs and grabbed the small suitcase Elena had packed for the hospital. When she got back downstairs, Elena was screaming again.

"I've called the doctor," Carmen said. "She's going to meet us at the hospital. You'll be all right with the others, won't you?" She took the suitcase and left the room without waiting for an answer.

"Of course." When the contraction was over, Zita helped Elena out of her chair and through the front door to the car that Carmen had waiting. Elena climbed inside and Zita strapped her in. Moments later, they were gone.

Zita sighed. Elena would be fine, she was sure, but life was going to get a little more hectic in the next couple of days with another baby in the house. She walked back inside into the living room, where Julio was still crying and Beatriz was close to tears herself. She gave Bea a hug. "It's all right. The pain is part of labor. Elena's going to be fine. We'll go and visit her when the baby arrives, but right now we should get some work done. Why don't you go clean your teeth and we'll start the lessons?"

"OK."

Zita took Julio from Teresa. "Thank you." She clucked and soothed the baby boy while Teresa and Beatriz got ready. When he'd calmed, she put him in his rocker and gave him a toy to play with. Then she began to teach.

***

By the end of the day Zita was exhausted. Julio had been grizzly all day and she discovered he was teething. She'd had to dig through all the baby things they had from one of the previous foster babies to find a teething ring. It quietened him down for a little while, long enough for her to take the girls through their English lessons. They'd both picked up the language quickly and were almost ready for school. She would have to talk to the Office of Refugee Resettlement and see if she could get them into the local school.

Checking the time, she called her mother to check how Elena was.

"We're almost there," Carmen said. In the background Zita heard moans and screams. "We can see the baby's head. Push *niñita!*"

Zita held the phone away from her ear as Carmen yelled encouragement to Elena. "Call me back," she said and hung up. A few minutes later the phone rang. "She is here," Carmen sobbed.

Zita smiled, tears in her own eyes. "Are they both all right?"

"*Sí.* They are fine."

"We'll give mama and baby a chance to rest. Can we visit after dinner?"

"Of course."

Zita hung up and turned to Beatriz and Teresa, who were waiting next to her. "Elena's had a baby girl. Both mama and baby are doing fine."

Beatriz closed her eyes and said a prayer of thanks.

"We'll visit after dinner." Which she should start making. The other girls had arrived home from school and were doing their homework, and Julio was finally sleeping. "Can you pick me some beans?" she asked Beatriz.

The girl nodded and headed outside.

Zita went into the kitchen and Teresa followed.

"Any news about my family?" she asked.

Zita shook her head, feeling bad for her. "We're still waiting for your mother to go to the office in the city and fill out the paperwork for asylum."

"Could you call them again?" Her voice was quiet, pleading.

Zita couldn't refuse. "I don't want to risk making your father suspicious, but I'll call Fernando and ask if he's been in contact."

Teresa beamed at her.

She dialed the number and Fernando answered. "*Hola.* It's Zita. How are things?"

"I was going to call you tomorrow. Johanna submitted all of the paperwork today. Now we have to wait for it to be processed."

Zita put her hand over the receiver and told Teresa. The girl burst into tears. Zita hugged her. "That's great news. Thank you for your help."

"It's my pleasure."

Zita hung up and handed Teresa a tissue.

"They'll be here soon, won't they?" Teresa said.

"I hope so." She wouldn't make promises she couldn't keep. So much could happen between now and when the application was approved. "Why don't you go and wash up? Dinner won't be long."

"OK," Teresa said and walked out.

Zita breathed out, pressing her palms into her eyes to stop the tears. This was the worst part. The waiting, the uncertainty. Teresa hadn't even received her own approval to stay. Her hearing was a couple of weeks away and they were still putting together evidence to prove her story. Fernando had helped, as he was quietly building a case against the gang who had captured her.

In the meantime, there was nothing else Zita could do.

With a sigh, she turned her attention to dinner.

***

It was Friday before Zita had a chance to investigate law school. She'd been too busy caring for the girls and a teething Julio, and double checking that everything was in place for new baby Xaviera. Carmen had spent most of her days at the hospital with Elena, supporting her and teaching her about baby care.

Zita hadn't even had much time to talk to David, who had called a couple of times, but generally during the rush that was dinner time. They had arranged to go out on Saturday night and she couldn't wait.

The house was now quiet and the girls were all in bed. Zita switched on her laptop and searched for law school entry requirements. As she read through the information she discovered there was a law school admission test she had to do for entry, and there was one coming up in a couple of weeks.

It had been such a long time since she'd sat a test. Her skin tightened thinking about it. After her mother had begun fostering girls, Zita had had little time to study, and now there was even less time in her day.

She'd probably fail. But if she didn't tell anyone about the test, no one would ever know. She'd only disappoint herself.

And if she didn't register, she'd disappoint herself anyway.

She took a deep breath and filled in the registration form. Then she downloaded the sample questions. She had to be positive. She tutored the girls every day, she just needed to tutor herself as well.

Zita opened the first document.

She *could* do this.

Chapter 8

David couldn't wait to see Zita again. She'd sounded so stressed and busy during the week that he wanted to get her away from Casa Flanagan. With that in mind, something low key was in order for their date. Dinner somewhere quiet and a movie. He was picking her up this time, so he'd booked a restaurant near to where she lived on the outskirts of Houston and checked the local movie theaters for what was showing.

In keeping with the casual date, he dressed in jeans and his favorite leather jacket and went to pick her up.

As he pulled into the address she'd given him, he stared. The house was huge, two stories high, and surrounded by a myriad of tropical plants. The property had to be a couple of acres at least, and there was an orchard and a few cottages next to the main house. It was very homey. The front door flew open and Carmen strode out, heading for the van that was parked to one side. She was quickly followed by a teenager holding a baby, and both were crying. Zita was right behind them, helping them into the car. He pulled over so not to block the driveway as Carmen tore down it.

"What's wrong?" he asked Zita as he got out of the car.

Zita sighed. "Julio has a fever. Alejandra is convinced he's going to die, and Mama's taking them to the hospital."

Concerned, he asked, "Is he going to be all right?"

"I suspect it's to do with his teething and he'll be fine, but if it's one thing we Salvadorans know, it's how to be emotional." She ran a hand through her hair. "Welcome to Casa Flanagan."

Her eyes were shadowed and her posture slumped. She was almost defeated. David pulled her into his arms and hugged her. "Rough week?"

"Yeah." She squeezed him and then stepped back. "I'm so sorry, David. I'm not going to be able to go out tonight. I need to look after the girls."

"Aren't they old enough to take care of themselves?" They were teenagers, and his parents had left him alone at that age.

"Elena's just home with her new baby and she shouldn't be left alone. She's too nervous still."

Disappointment curled in his stomach. He wasn't used to dating someone with these kinds of responsibilities. He'd been looking forward to getting her away and spending time with her. "I could stay here, help you with the girls." How hard could it be?

"I can't ask you to do that. It's a madhouse today."

David shrugged. "You didn't ask, I offered." He took her hand and led her toward the house. "I can go get food for dinner, and we can keep an eye on the girls together." What time did teenagers normally go to bed?

She stared at him for a long moment. "I'm not sure you understand what you're getting yourself in for, but I'm so tired I'm going to say yes."

His stomach rolled over at her ominous tone.

It took about five seconds for David to realize Zita hadn't been kidding about the madhouse. The girls were gathered in the living room, and as Zita walked in they started speaking rapidly in Spanish.

Their voices got higher and louder as the argument continued. One girl, who he assumed was Elena because she was holding a tiny baby, looked fearful and was angling the baby away from the group. A younger girl, perhaps Beatriz, hovered around her.

Each girl spoke over the other, without taking a breath, getting more and more worked up.

He glanced toward the entrance. He was way out of his

depth.

"Enough!" Zita yelled and the girls shut up. "Julio is going to be fine. His fever is probably related to his teething, which is something every baby goes through. Elena, you don't need to worry about Xaviera catching anything. She's crying because she's hungry, not because she's sick. Now, it's time we all ate. Mama prepared some chili before she left. Larissa, set the table, and the rest of you wash up."

To David's relief, the girls all left to do what Zita had told them, with the exception of Elena, who stood crying in the center of the room. "I didn't know Xaviera was hungry. I'm a bad mother."

Oh hell. He hated tears.

Zita went over to the young girl and led her to the sofa. "Sit down."

She did, clutching her baby to her chest.

"You're a new mama, so it will take a while for you to distinguish the cries and learn the signs. I know because I've been through it with Julio and several other babies over the years. When they're so young, all they do is eat, cry and sleep. Now, is your milk flowing all right?"

"Yes." Elena lifted up one side of her top to start breastfeeding.

David glanced away, staring at the family photos on the opposite wall. What was he supposed to do now? Hang around here with Zita while not looking at the breastfeeding mother? Was it all right to acknowledge her breastfeeding or should he ignore it completely? He didn't know the conventions for this kind of thing.

"David, do you want to help me dish up?"

Relief poured through him at the escape she provided. "Yes." He followed her into the kitchen.

"Breastfeeding is a perfectly natural and normal thing," Zita commented as she turned on the stove.

"I know," he said. "But where am I supposed to look?"

"The baby's head covers most of the breast, so you don't need to worry. Looking at Elena is fine. If she was uncomfortable she would have gone out of the room to feed, but in Guatemala no one makes a fuss about these things."

"I haven't spent a lot of time around babies."

"I can tell," Zita said with a grin.

He laughed. "That obvious, huh?" He was fascinated by how calm and patient Zita was, particularly with how tired she was. "So you've had a lot of experience with this?"

"Five babies so far," she said. "We help those who want to keep the child and arrange adoptions if necessary." She stirred the pot of chili.

It was another aspect of the immigration process he'd not known about. As the girls gathered in the dining room, he asked, "Can I help with anything?"

"Can you grab the jug of iced tea from the refrigerator?" Rich aromas of chili filled the air and David sniffed in appreciation as he did as she asked.

When they were all sitting down, and Zita had introduced him, she said grace and they started eating.

"Have you got any homework this weekend?" Zita asked.

Larissa grimaced. "Math and English."

"Same here," Tiana said.

"Do you need any help?"

David smiled. He remembered his father asking if he'd done his homework, though he couldn't recall any offer of help.

"The math is difficult. I don't understand it," Larissa complained.

"Neither do I," Zita muttered. "We'll work it out together."

"I can help," David offered. "Numbers are my thing," he reminded Zita when she stared at him.

"That would be great," she said. "It won't take nearly as long with you helping."

Elena came into the room, holding Xaviera.

"Let me take her while you eat," Zita said, getting to her feet and taking the baby from Elena.

"Thank you."

The baby was calm now, her eyes wide as she lay in Zita's arms. She was so unbelievably tiny, with her arms and legs tucked up in the blanket.

Zita glanced at David as she sat back down. "Do you want to hold her?"

"Hell no." He held his hands up. "I'd probably break her,

she's so small."

The girls laughed at him.

"You get used to it," Elena said, dishing herself up some chili.

"Not up to the challenge?" Zita teased him.

"Nope," David said, quite happy to admit he was out of his depth. But Zita wasn't. The way she rocked the baby was unconscious and natural. She'd obviously had plenty of practice. She'd make a good mother one day.

He flinched. He did not want to think about motherhood and the woman he was dating in the same sentence. Parenthood was a long way off as far as he was concerned.

After the table was cleared and the dishes stacked in the dishwasher, David sat at the dining table with Larissa and Tiana. The television was on in the next room and it sounded like a reality show. Larissa was listening.

"Do you like the show?" David asked her.

"It's a good way to learn English," she said. "People on those shows talk like normal people and they talk fast. It is hard to understand at first, but gets easier with practice."

He hadn't thought of it that way before. The different accents in the States must make it difficult for those learning English.

"This is what I'm stuck with," Tiana said when she'd unpacked her books and notepad.

David turned to her and focused on the problem.

An hour later, the math work was done, and Tiana and Larissa had moved on to English. Zita was upstairs putting Beatriz to bed, so David went into the living room where Teresa and Elena were now watching a different show. Teresa eyed him somewhat warily, so he took a seat on the opposite side of the room.

It was easy for him to forget what had happened to the girls. They appeared like any other teenagers until they were alone with him. Then their fear reminded him how they'd been abused. He couldn't imagine living with that every day.

When Zita came back downstairs, she was holding a phone

to her ear. "That's good news. I'll tell the girls." She hung up. "Julio is fine. The doctors gave him some pain relief and his temperature is coming down. They're keeping him there for another hour for observation and then they'll be home."

Elena crossed herself. *"Gracias a Dios."*

Zita's shoulders were slumped and her eyes were a little dull.

"Come, sit down." David patted the spot next to him.

She complied, sinking onto the sofa with a sigh.

He pulled her close and massaged her shoulders. "You're very tense."

"Oh, don't do that. You'll put me to sleep." She leaned into the massage, belying her words.

He continued to rub the knots in her back. "You need to relax."

She didn't say another word, but slowly, her muscles relaxed. The show ended and the girls said goodnight and went upstairs to bed.

Zita sat up. "I'm sorry about tonight. I was looking forward to our date."

"It's fine. I still got to hang out with you." He felt good about being useful and had a real appreciation for what she actually did here.

"I bet you didn't picture your night involving algebra and crying babies," she said with a small smile.

"Not exactly," he admitted. "But it was fun. The girls are great. Why you ever said what you do isn't work, I don't know. You're like a mother to all of these girls, and that's got to be one of the hardest jobs there is."

"Mama usually does all the work. I just help out."

"That's not what I saw."

"But do you understand why I can't leave her alone? If there wasn't someone else here, who would have cared for the girls tonight?"

"Both Larissa and Tiana are old enough to care for the others, and I'm sure if Daniella was home, she would have come over. You said she lived on the property, right?"

She nodded. "The girls wouldn't have known what to do with Xaviera."

"They would have figured it out if it had come to that."

Perhaps he was being too optimistic. He knew nothing about babies, but his first thought would have been food and then to check its diaper. "Besides, Carly said there was money for a caregiver, didn't she?"

"Yes," she admitted.

"Have you investigated law school?"

"Yeah, I registered to do the LSA test, which is in a couple of weeks."

"That's great. What happens when you pass?"

"If I get a high enough score, I might get straight in with my experience." She shrugged. "If not, I need to enroll into college." She shifted a little more on the seat.

"Awesome." He pulled her closer and kissed her. He loved the way she melted into him.

Somewhere in the house, a door slammed shut. "Sounds like Mama's home," Zita said, sitting up.

Sure enough, a few minutes later Carmen came into the living room with Alejandra holding a sleeping Julio.

David stood up with Zita.

"How is he?" Zita asked.

"He'll be fine. Everyone's a little tired," Carmen said. Alejandra continued upstairs with her baby. Carmen nodded to David. "I didn't get a chance to say hello to you earlier."

"You had bigger concerns," he said. She looked as tired as Zita. "You all need a good night's sleep. I'd better be going."

Zita took hold of his hand. "I'll walk you out."

"You're more than welcome to stay," Carmen said. "It's late and you've got a long drive home." She went upstairs.

OK, that was weird. He'd been invited to stay by his date's mother.

Zita squeezed his hand. "You can stay if you want. My bed's big enough for two, but I thought you might feel awkward."

There was such sadness in her eyes and he wanted it to go away. He wanted to hold her and make her feel better. It was a strange feeling. "I'd love to stay."

She smiled then, big and bright. He felt like a hero.

"Come on then." She took his hand and they climbed the stairs.

***

David groaned as a baby's cries woke him. This time at least it was light outside, but the other four times during the night it hadn't been. No wonder Zita was so damn tired. At least twice she'd got up to help and now she was stirring in her sleep again.

He snuggled into her and whispered, "It's not time to get up yet."

She mumbled something in her sleep and settled back down. Outside the room, there were loud voices in Spanish. One sounded upset, the other angry.

Zita stirred again.

No, she needed to sleep. Carefully, he got out of bed and dressed and checked his hair in Zita's mirror, before slipping outside. Maybe there was something he could do to help, even if it was just to make breakfast, so they could take their argument downstairs away from Zita.

Alejandra was standing with her hands on her hips, glaring at Elena who was holding a crying Xaviera.

"Morning," he said.

The shock on the girls' faces would have been comical if it hadn't been accompanied by a split second of fear as well. He stopped where he was, keeping his distance, and gave his friendliest smile.

"Is something wrong?"

"She won't take her baby downstairs. Her crying is going to wake Julio," Alejandra said.

"*Mamita* said I could stay in bed today," Elena said. "I'm so tired."

"We're all tired, but you're a mother now. You have to be strong," Alejandra told her.

Before Elena retorted, David asked, "Has Xaviera been fed?"

Elena nodded.

"Changed?"

She nodded again.

That ruled out what he knew about babies. "Why don't I take her downstairs for a walk?" he suggested, thinking only to get the crying baby away from Zita. "You can go back to sleep."

"Do you know anything about babies?" Alejandra asked, at the same time that Elena said, "All right."

Alejandra flounced back into her own room as Elena handed him the crying bundle. *Shit.* The baby was tiny, her neck kind of floppy, and he used one hand to brace it. He forced a smile to his face. "I've got this." He wasn't sure who he was trying to convince, Elena or himself. She went back into her bedroom and he moved toward the stairs, walking slowly.

Hell, when had stairs become a trap for the unwary? They were so steep. One false step and he'd tumble down them, baby in his arms. He couldn't use the banister because both hands were occupied by Xaviera. He inched his way to the bottom, sweating profusely.

Praying Carmen was in the kitchen, he headed there, but the kitchen was empty. He gently shushed Xaviera, swaying the way Zita had at dinner the previous night. It didn't have any effect. He glanced around and spotted a folded stroller in the laundry, but one look showed him it was going to be much too complicated to work out while holding a baby. A baby that was surprisingly getting heavier the longer he held her.

Walking over to the window, he peered outside. It was overcast, but not raining. Perhaps some fresh air would be good. He managed to hold the baby and support her head with one hand, while he quickly opened the back door and stepped outside. There was a bit of a chill in the air, but Xaviera was bundled up. To be on the safe side, he wrapped one side of his leather jacket around her as well.

He was a few steps along the path before his mind registered what he was seeing.

The garden was amazing. In every direction there were lush green plants falling over each other in a competition as to which was the most beautiful. It was a jungle begging to be explored.

With a grin, he wandered down the path to see what he could find.

***

Zita woke from a lovely dream starring David. She rolled over and stretched, reaching for him so she could reenact it. The other side of her bed was empty.

David had stayed the night. She was sure of it.

But where was he?

Quickly, she got up and dressed. The house was surprisingly silent. Maybe the others had gone to the early session of church. She hurried downstairs and found her mother in the kitchen making coffee. "Have you seen David this morning?"

"Yes, he's out in the garden with Xaviera."

Zita frowned as she headed outside. What was he doing with the baby? He wouldn't even hold her last night. "David," she called.

"Over here."

His response was hardly more than a whisper. Following the sound, she found him seated on one of the garden benches, Xaviera cradled in his arms and his jacket half covering her to keep her warm. Her heart stuttered at the sweet picture. "What are you doing?"

"Shh. She's just gone to sleep."

Zita pressed her lips together to stop from smiling at his slightly panicked tone. She lowered her voice. "How long have you been out here?"

"I don't know. It was about seven when I got up."

It was now eight o'clock. "How come you have Xaviera?"

"She was crying and Elena and Alejandra were arguing. I didn't want them to wake you, so I offered to take her downstairs. Then I wasn't sure whether you'd still be able to hear her in the kitchen, so I brought her outside."

Zita's heart melted. He'd taken care of the baby so she could sleep a little longer. She bent over and kissed him. "Thank you."

He smiled. "You're welcome."

"Why don't you come inside and I'll cook you a big breakfast? You deserve it."

He hesitated, glancing down at the baby. "I don't want to wake her."

Zita did chuckle then. "She'll be fine. The house is quiet and babies can sleep through all sorts of things."

He peered at Xaviera again.

"I promise," Zita said. "Besides, it's cold out here."

"All right."

Inch by inch, he got to his feet. Zita swallowed her laughter.

He had no experience with babies, which made him doubly sweet for doing this.

"This garden is incredible," he said quietly as they walked back to the house.

"It's Mama's passion," she said.

When they got inside, David insisted on putting Xaviera in the stroller so Elena could sleep longer too, so Zita set it up. He carefully laid the baby inside, freezing in place when she stirred for a moment. Then he pushed the stroller into the living room where it was warmer and they'd hear her if she stirred.

When he was happy, Zita started breakfast. His heroics deserved the full *Desayuno Salvadoreno*, and the girls would enjoy it as well. Through the doorway, she saw her mother sitting at the dining table, drinking a coffee and reading the newspaper.

"Mama, I'm making *Desayuno Salvadoreno*. Do you want some?"

"*Sí. Gracias.*"

Zita poured David a coffee and pointed to a stool. "Sit down and rest your arms."

He grinned. "They get heavy, don't they?"

"Sure do. Next time I'll show you how to use the baby sling." She grabbed the ingredients she needed from the fridge.

"Can I help?" he asked.

"Nope. You got extra brownie points for letting me sleep in, so you can sit there and look pretty while I cook you a meal."

"If I'd known all I needed to do was hold a baby to get you to cook for me, I would have done it sooner."

She laughed. "It was incredibly brave of you." And for that she kissed him again, this time a little longer. "You're my hero."

Beatriz came charging into the room. "I'm hungry."

Zita smiled at the young girl. "Can you feed Bess and Saint for me, and I'll make you breakfast?"

"All right."

After she'd fed the dogs, Beatriz and David chatted while Zita cooked. David slowed his speech to make it easier for her to understand. Beatriz was telling him about Guatemala and why she had left. Zita had heard the story before, but it didn't make it any easier. The girl's stepfather deserved to rot in hell.

By the time Zita had finished cooking, the rest of the girls had appeared. Zita dished up and handed a plate to David. "Traditional Salvadoran breakfast – scrambled eggs, tortillas, pureed beans, fried plaintains and sour cream."

"Thank you. It smells great."

They all moved into the dining room. As Zita sat next to David, she asked Alejandra, "How is Julio this morning?"

"Much better."

"*Mamita*, can Larissa and I go to the mall today?" Tiana asked. "We wanted to meet a couple of friends."

"Boy friends or girl friends?" Carmen asked.

"Both," Larissa answered.

Zita was silent. She wanted to spend some time alone with David today, but she couldn't see how it would be possible. Carmen would want to stay at home with the babies, which meant she'd have to take the girls to the mall if Carmen said yes.

"You will have to ask Zita if she can take you."

Both girls turned their pleading eyes on Zita. Hell, how could she say no? She glanced at David. "What have you got planned for today?"

He shrugged. "If we go to the mall we could watch the movie we missed last night."

She blinked. "You wouldn't mind?"

"No. I haven't been to a mall in ages." He smiled at her.

She couldn't believe he wasn't a little bit ticked off about having to share her. None of her previous boyfriends had wanted to know much about her family. "All right."

"Thanks, David," the girls chimed.

She squeezed his hands. "Thank you."

"No problem. It's going to be fun."

She hoped so.

Chapter 9

Going to the mall wasn't the ideal way David wanted to spend the day, but after seeing how much Tiana and Larissa wanted to go, he understood why Zita couldn't say no. They were normal teenagers wanting to meet up with friends, and it showed how far they'd come from fleeing for their lives. Besides, he was still spending time with Zita.

After breakfast, he drove them all to the mall. The girls had insisted they take his car. He couldn't blame them. The black mustang was impressive.

After he parked, Larissa and Tiana hurried to their designated meeting spot with promises they would be ready to go by three.

Zita took hold of his hand. "Where to first?"

"I need to buy a fresh shirt." He'd sweated a lot while holding Xaviera and didn't want to smell.

"Of course. I should have thought."

They headed for the nearest menswear shop. As David browsed, he asked Zita, "What's the latest with Teresa's case?"

"Her mother and sister have applied for asylum and are waiting for it to be processed. Teresa's hearing is in a couple of weeks."

"They're still in El Salvador, right?" He held up a green shirt, but decided he didn't like the color. He put it down.

She nodded. "We're trying to speed along the processing, as

it's dangerous for them."

"How so?"

"The gang took Teresa's little sister as punishment for Teresa running away. If they find out Manuela and Johanna have applied for asylum, they'll punish or kill them both."

He froze. "Kill them for moving away?"

"For defying the gang."

Damn. Here he was worried about a new shirt when their lives were on the line. "How quickly can it be processed?" He took the shirt he was holding to the cash register.

"It's supposed to take no more than forty-five days until the interview, but there's a backlog. Then it can take up to one hundred and eighty days for a decision to be made."

Anything could happen in that time. "Surely it won't take so long in Teresa's case? It's obvious she was abused and is in danger."

Zita shrugged. "I don't know. Not many of the foster girls apply for asylum. Both Fernando and Mama have flagged it as urgent, so it might help."

David hoped so. If his father was serious about politics, maybe he could speed up the processing time. He'd have to speak to him about it. "So what about Beatriz and Elena?"

"Beatriz's hearing is tomorrow, but Elena doesn't have a date yet."

"Can anybody go to it?"

Zita looked at him. "No. It's closed to the public because Beatriz has been abused, but if you're interested, I can tell you what happens."

"Yeah, I'd like that." The more he knew the better.

After David changed his shirt, they headed for the movie theater. There weren't many people in there at that time of the day. He wrapped his arm around Zita's shoulder and she leaned into him. She fit so well against him and was so comfortable with giving affection. Having her next to him made him feel important. Pressing a kiss against her hair, he settled in to watch.

"That was amazing," Zita said, her eyes shining as they exited the theater a couple of hours later.

David kissed her. He loved seeing her happy and relaxed. "It sure was. Do you want to get some lunch?"

"Yeah. Let me just check my phone and make sure the girls haven't texted me." She dug through her bag until she found her cell and checked. "A message from Mama." She was silent as she read it. She sighed. "It's a grocery list. We'll have to pick up a few things before we head home." Her expression was apologetic.

"Fine by me." It was a new experience to be so needed, but it was kind of nice. His family was so independent that it would never occur to him to ask them for anything.

"You really are easy to please," Zita said.

"I'm happy as long as I'm spending time with you." The words were out before he thought about them. It was true, though, and that was scary. They'd only been on a couple of dates. He'd never been so invested in a relationship before.

Zita stared at him, her mouth agape. He should backpedal, he probably sounded mad. Before he could, she launched herself into his arms and kissed him.

"That's the nicest thing anyone has ever said to me." She kissed him again. "I like hanging out with you too."

Relief flooded him and he held her tightly, enjoying the way her body fit against his. "Good to know."

She wiggled out of his hold. "We should cut down on the public display of affection. People are glaring at us."

He didn't care what people thought, which was new for him. "They're just jealous." He kissed her again and then took her hand. "What do you want to eat?"

"There's an Irish pub outside."

"Sounds good."

Inside the pub David was immediately transported to Dublin. There were wooden floors, sturdy wooden tables and chairs, and a well-stocked bar with a sign proclaiming the best Guinness in America. They found a table and Zita sighed.

"Are you all right?"

She smiled. "This place always reminds me of Papa. He probably drank at a pub like this before he left Ireland."

"Is that where he's from?"

"Yeah. He came to El Salvador in his early twenties and never left. He died when I was three."

"Is that why when you swear, you say 'feck'?"

She blushed. "Yes. It started when I was a teenager and desperately wanted a connection to Papa. I thought if I used the occasional Irish phrase, I'd be honoring his memory, keeping some part of him alive." She shrugged. "Now it's a habit."

"I can understand." It would be hard to lose a parent so young. "Do you have much contact with his family in Ireland?"

"I don't have any. He was an only child and his parents died before I was born."

"What about extended family?"

"None that I know of. I was going to look into it this year." She grimaced. "But I haven't found the time."

They placed their orders.

"Maybe you should set some more time-based goals."

She screwed up her face. "You're right. I'll set them when I get home." She typed something into her phone. "So what have you got planned next weekend? Maybe we can do something together — just the two of us."

"I have the guys coming around for poker on Friday night." He normally looked forward to it, but now he kind of wished he had the evening free.

"Which guys are these?"

"My college friends. We get together once a month to play poker and tell lies."

She laughed. "Tell me more. Did you get up to lots of mischief?"

"A bit." He grinned, taking a sip of his wine. "Garth was my roommate, and we were taking the same classes as Lee and Colin."

"I wouldn't have picked accounting majors as being mischief makers."

"How little you know." He'd meant it as a joke but her face fell.

"You're right. I've not been to college."

He covered her hand. "I wasn't implying you were dumb."

She shrugged. "I know. I haven't had the experience. It doesn't matter."

But it clearly did. Their food arrived and Zita started eating. David didn't know what to say to cheer her up.

Zita's phone buzzed. Checking the message she said, "The girls will be ready by half past two. We should hurry so we can get the groceries before then."

"All right." She clearly didn't want to talk about it, so he changed the subject.

***

The weekend hadn't been so bad after all. Zita was certain she would have scared David off after the crazy at her place, but he'd barely been fazed by it. Then he'd said he was happy spending time with her, and her heart had melted a little.

"Zita, are you ready?" Carmen called.

"Coming." She had to focus on what she was supposed to be doing. Today was Beatriz's final hearing.

Zita checked her appearance, making sure her braid was still tidy and her dark skirt suit was free of dog hair. Stopping by Beatriz's bedroom, she found the ten year old sitting on the edge of her bed, chewing her lip and playing with the buttons on her shirt.

"How are you feeling, Bea?" Zita asked.

The girl looked up at her, her eyes fearful. "What if they send me home? Pablo will kill me for running away."

Zita's heart squeezed. She couldn't promise the girl a positive outcome, all she said was, "We're going to do everything we can to convince them to let you stay." She hugged her. "We should get going."

Beatriz slipped her hand into Zita's. She swallowed. God, she hated this bit. She felt everything her sisters felt. The fear of them being sent back to their dangerous homeland would be suffocating if she let it overwhelm her. Instead of letting it show, Zita kept up a constant chatter about Xaviera and Elena. At the front door, she waited while her mother and the girls wished Beatriz luck, and then they got into her car and drove into Houston.

The hearing was being held at the immigration court. Zita and Beatriz met Shelly outside the building, and together they went through the security checks and then into the waiting room for their case to be called. Zita was allowed into the courtroom as Beatriz's guardian.

"We have all the evidence to present," Shelly told Beatriz. "You have a strong case."

She was encouraging, but Zita only heard what she wasn't saying. There was no guarantee Beatriz would be allowed to stay in the country. Her stomach swirled as she tried not to picture having to put Beatriz on a plane back to her stepfather.

"Beatriz Morales," a clerk called.

Zita and Shelly stood. Zita took hold of the young girl's hand. "Come on, Bea."

Her hand was shaking. She gave a small nod as they followed the clerk into the courtroom and took their seats behind one of the desks. At the other desk sat the lawyer representing the Department of Homeland Security. It was his job to ensure those people who were suspected of being a danger to the United States weren't permitted to remain in the country. If they had examined the evidence impartially, Beatriz *should* be allowed to stay. But there was always a first time.

Judge Torres began the proceedings by turning on the recording equipment and going through the identification of all those present. The only other person in the room was the interpreter who would translate for Beatriz.

When the evidence was presented to the judge — photos of Beatriz bruised and beaten, and statements they had received from her mother and neighbors in Guatemala — the DHS lawyer made his first objection.

"These are not strong pieces of evidence," he said. "There is nothing stopping the mother or neighbors from lying in their statements, and there is no proof the injuries were in actual fact caused by the respondent's stepfather. She could have been in a fight with gang members."

Zita gritted her teeth. Logically, she knew he was right, but he hadn't sat with Beatriz as she'd relived the terror, hadn't yet heard her stories of how she had hidden every time Pablo had come home from work, particularly if he'd been drinking. He hadn't listened as Beatriz told of trying to fight him off, of being thrown across the room and threatened with death.

Zita didn't listen as Shelly responded to the accusations. She'd been through this so many times, the only thing that was different was the girl sitting next to her. She squeezed Beatriz's hand as the interpreter kept Beatriz informed about what was being said.

Finally, it was Bea's turn to speak. Zita had been coaching her over the past few weeks, making sure she knew what information she needed to tell the judge. The girl shook as she stood and held onto Zita's hand tightly. She spoke softly at first, hesitant, and as Shelly asked her further questions she grew more confident in her responses. When it came time to talk about the abuse, she stopped.

"You can do this," Zita told her in Spanish.

The girl nodded and told the judge about living with Pablo. Tears ran down her face as she recounted the abuse, the fear and the desperation, which had led to her leaving the country with Elena.

Zita blinked back her own tears, swallowing hard to get her emotions under control. She needed to be strong.

When Beatriz was done and all the questions and cross-examination was completed, the judge was silent as she reviewed her notes.

Zita hugged Bea, keeping an eye on the judge. She could render her decision immediately, or she could postpone it.

The judge cleared her throat. "In the matter of Beatriz Morales' application for relief from removal, I hereby grant her relief. Beatriz may stay in the United States."

Zita didn't listen to the rest. She hugged Beatriz. "You're staying," she said. "You're staying with us."

Beatriz burst into tears and Zita held the girl tightly. She ushered them out of the room and thanked Shelly.

"It's my pleasure. The DHS has a couple of weeks to lodge an appeal, but I don't think they'll do that. In the meantime, you know what you need to do from here, don't you, Zita?"

"Yes." She'd been through the documentation requirements many times over the past few years.

"I think you know it better than I do," Shelly laughed. "If you had formal qualifications, you wouldn't need me at all."

Zita smiled. She wanted to talk to Shelly about that, but not while Beatriz was here. "I'll be in touch."

They said their goodbyes and Zita called her mother.

"How did it go?"

"Application was approved. Beatriz is staying." She held the cell away from her ear as her mother shrieked in delight. Beatriz giggled. "We'll be home soon. I'll pick up something for dinner so we can celebrate."

"Good idea."

Zita hung up and put an arm around Beatriz. "Come on, *niñita*. We've got a celebration to organize."

***

David checked his calendar and breathed a sigh of relief. No meetings for at least three hours. That had to be a record. He hated sitting in those rooms, wasting time talking about things without any decisions being made. There had to be a better way. But each time he brought it up with his father, he was ignored.

He glanced at his screen. He had to finish a report he'd been trying to complete all last week. It was one of those mind-numbing chores that had to be done and he hated it. If he was honest, there wasn't much he enjoyed about his job. Zita's question the other day had really made him stop and think. He'd love a job where he was challenged, where he had the freedom to do what he wanted, where he was in charge. At college, he'd briefly considered creating his own consultancy firm — he liked coming up with ideas and making them happen — but he'd known even then that he'd had no choice.

He shook his head. There was no point dreaming. He put on his headphones, choosing the rock playlist on his phone, turned it up loud, and got to work.

As soon as he opened the spreadsheet, something nudged his shoulder. He turned, taking the headphones off, and was confronted with a scowling father. He smiled. "Bob."

"You can't hear a damned thing with those things on. I've been standing here talking to you and you haven't heard a word."

"My apologies." David stopped the music. "What can I do for you?" He gestured to a chair, but Bob remained standing.

"I'm running for governor."

David's eyebrows rose. "Congratulations."

"I'll announce it next month, and you'll become acting CEO.

You need to get one of your team members up to speed to fill in for you."

That was fast, way too fast for David's comfort. His stomach started churning. Should he tell his father he didn't want to take over?

No, he couldn't. There was no other succession plan, and he couldn't leave his father in the lurch.

"You've been following a couple of migrant cases, haven't you?" Bob asked.

"Yeah." He pushed his concern aside and reached for the file where he was recording his thoughts and research on the immigration process.

"Good." Bob took the file from him and flicked through it. He nodded, and handed it back. "It's going to be one of my main policies."

David smiled. "That's great. I wanted to talk to you about it. The assessment process takes too long. There's a family in El Salvador who are in danger, but it could be six months before their application is processed."

"They should go to their own government for help."

David leaned back in surprise. "It's not that —"

"But I agree with the lengthy process," Bob continued. "It should be quick — process them and send them home." He checked his watch. "I've got to run. We'll talk about this more later. The information you're gathering will be useful." He strode out of the room.

David stared after him. His father had it all wrong. He couldn't possibly believe it was so cut and dried.

Shaking his head, he opened the file. Maybe he hadn't made it clear. He'd go through it again, add some more detail and then sit down with Bob and explain. Make sure he understood.

His cell rang and he checked the display. "Hi, Zita."

"Hey! We're celebrating tonight. Beatriz's application was approved, which means she gets to stay in the States. Do you want to come for dinner?"

"Sure. That's fantastic news." He was so pleased. After hearing her story, he would have hated her to have to return home.

"Can you be here by six-thirty?"

"Yeah." He'd leave work a little early. The prospect of seeing Zita when he hadn't expected to was exciting.

"If you want, you can stay the night."

He hesitated. It was kind of weird to stay at Carmen's house, but it did mean he got to spend more time with Zita. "All right. See you then."

David hung up and the immigration file caught his eye. He'd get some more information about Beatriz's case tonight and show his father how wrong he was. He'd change his stance when he knew the facts.

David was sure.

Chapter 10

Zita was practically floating when she arrived home with Beatriz. At the front door, Carmen and the girls crowded around Beatriz, hugging and congratulating her. Elena wasn't there, but she was probably with Xaviera. As Carmen fussed, Zita went into the kitchen and unpacked the groceries she'd bought on the way home. Tonight they would prepare a huge meal to celebrate with all of Beatriz's favorite foods: tamales, stuffed cucumbers and fried fritters.

Carmen walked in, wiping her eyes with the back of her sleeve.

"Happy, Mama?"

"*Sí.* Of course. It is such good news." She hugged Zita, holding her tightly. "We saved another one."

Tears welled up in Zita's eyes and a lump lodged in her throat. "We did," she whispered. This was why she did this. To give these girls a better chance at life. She swallowed. "Have you invited the others yet?"

Carmen nodded. "They will be here. I couldn't get in touch with Daniella, though."

"I'll go check her cabin," Zita said. "Her cell might have run flat again."

She walked outside, taking a deep breath and calming her emotions. Beatriz was safe and no longer needed to fear her stepfather. She would stay with them and grow up with the other girls. If Elena and Teresa were also accepted, that would be it for a while because they could only foster six girls at a time. This was one of the reasons studying law was so important. Zita would be able to help other immigrants who they weren't able to foster.

She stopped at Daniella's cabin and knocked. There was a murmur of voices inside before Daniella opened the door, adjusting her top. Zita glanced over Daniella's shoulder and saw a guy sitting at the table, seemingly engrossed in the notes strewn across it. She hid her smile as she said, "I hope I'm not disturbing you."

Daniella waved her hand, slightly flustered. "No, I was just studying."

Zita bet it wasn't all they were doing. "We're having a party over at the house if you want to come. Beatriz's application was approved."

"That's fantastic!" Daniella grinned. She glanced at the guy.

"You can bring your friend as well," Zita said.

"Ah, maybe."

Zita smiled. "Drop by any time." She left, walking slowly back through the garden. It was nice to see Daniella with a guy. It meant she was letting men back into her life, which she hadn't been able to do earlier.

Zita entered the kitchen where she found Carmen cooking and Beatriz sitting at the breakfast bar, nibbling on some chips. Elena walked in with Xaviera, and Beatriz jumped off her stool.

"Did you hear, Elena? They've approved my application! I'm staying!" She beamed and held her hands out to take Xaviera.

Elena scowled and shifted Xaviera away from Beatriz. "There's no need to brag," she said in Spanish. "It's insensitive. I should have never brought you with me."

Beatriz's face fell and her bottom lip trembled.

"Elena . . ." Carmen began.

Elena shoved Xaviera into Zita's arms and ran outside, crying.

Zita exchanged a look with her mother as she soothed the baby. It was understandable that Elena was upset, but she was taking her anger and fear out on Beatriz more often.

"I'll talk with her," Carmen said and followed Elena outside.

Moving over to Beatriz, Zita put an arm around her shoulders. "She didn't mean it, Bea," she said. "She's just emotional at the moment."

Beatriz brushed away the tears and nodded, climbing back onto the stool. "I should have thought. I won't say anything else."

"You're allowed to celebrate. I'm sure Elena will come around."

"I hope so." Bea looked so upset.

Zita sighed.

A couple of hours later, dinner was prepared and Bridget, Jack, Carly and Evan had arrived. Zita checked the time, just as Bess and Saint started barking. She hurried to the front door and opened it. David was getting out of his car. She grinned, thrilled he'd agreed to celebrate with them.

"Hi." She trotted down the steps and wrapped her arms around his neck, kissing him. The kiss sent warmth all the way to her toes and the tension of the last few hours dissolved. She stepped back.

"Hi." He smiled slowly. "I'm not late, am I?"

Zita needed a second to get her heart rate under control. "Not at all." She turned to go back inside, but he tugged her back and kissed her again. She wanted to drag him up to her room and have some alone time with him, but that would have to wait.

As they walked up the steps, he asked, "Would some of your foster sisters be willing to talk to me about their experiences?"

"I can ask. Why?"

"Dad's running for governor, and wants to make immigration one of his top priorities."

"In what way?" she asked. Bob Randall didn't appear to be someone who would be pro-immigration.

"He's got it wrong at the moment. I want to show him what you do at Casa Flanagan and how you help so many people."

"And you believe you'll be able to change his mind?"

"Of course. He's not unreasonable."

Zita debated whether to disagree with him. Bridget had had first-hand experience of how unreasonable Bob could be, and

Zita's own experience with him hadn't been that great. But David knew his father better than she did. "We can ask the girls tonight."

"Great."

She pushed aside her concern as they entered the house.

****

Zita had been busy over the past few days sorting out Beatriz's paperwork. She closed her bedroom door and exhaled. Every time she'd wanted to study for her LSAT, her mother was around and she couldn't risk Carmen asking what she was doing. She'd felt so guilty even reading the documents, but the test was only ten days away.

Firing up her laptop, she settled on her bed. Was there any point doing the test? The colleges she'd called suggested they would *consider* her application if her test scores were good enough, even though she had no undergraduate degree. The fact that she had so much experience with immigration law was a plus, but no guarantee. So she might be wasting her time.

She shook her head. It wasn't like her to be so pessimistic. Opening the preparation material she'd downloaded, she settled down to read.

After an hour, she rubbed her eyes. The reading comprehension section was dense and she was tired, but that was no excuse. The material she would have to read if she actually passed the test and got into law school would be far more complicated than this. And she would have much more work to do.

Did she really want to go through with this?

Was it worth the time and the effort?

Her mind wandered to the immigration courtroom and the expression on Beatriz's face when she understood she was safe. Yes, she did want to go through with this. She wanted to offer people like Beatriz hope, to fight for their right to live without fear.

Which meant she needed to focus.

She set the timer on her phone and started the next section.

A knock on her door startled Zita from her work. "Yes?"

The door opened and Carmen poked her head in. "Are you still up?"

Zita shut her screen quickly and said, "Just surfing the net." The guilt crept over her. Maybe she should tell her mother.

Carmen smiled. "Don't stay up too late. We've got the swap meet tomorrow."

Feck. She'd forgotten about it. She forced a smile on her face. "I won't. Night, Mama." Zita waited until Carmen had closed the door before opening the screen again. She should turn it off. It was already past midnight and she'd have to be up at six. On Friday mornings, they brought any excess produce from their garden to a market largely attended by migrants. It was a busy morning catching up with friends and helping those who needed it.

There wasn't a lot more she was going to take in tonight anyway.

Switching off her computer, she then snuggled under her covers and went to sleep.

***

David really looked forward to poker night with his friends, and after the day he'd had he needed a drink as well. He poured a bag of chips into a bowl, and then added a selection of antipasto to the table. Poker night was always held at his place now, because his three friends were all married, and Lee even had a baby on the way.

He opened a bottle of wine to breathe and checked the time. His doorbell rang. It had to be Colin, he was right on time.

Answering the door, he found both Colin and Garth standing there.

"Randy Randall," Garth greeted him. "How's it going?"

David scowled at the nickname. "Cut it out and come in." As he was about to shut the door, the elevator dinged and Lee stepped out.

"Damn, I thought I was going to beat Colin this time," Lee said, winking at him.

"Never gonna happen," Colin stated. "Unless of course you're early."

David grinned at his friends. Colin's punctuality had been a running gag since college.

"What's new?" he asked, handing Lee and Garth bottles of beer and pouring Colin and himself a glass of wine each.

"Mom and Dad are handing the business over to me," Colin said and sipped his wine.

David raised his eyebrows. "Is one of them sick?" None of them ever thought Colin's parents would let go of the accounting firm they ran.

"No. They decided on an early retirement. They're going back to Hong Kong for a few months to visit with family and then they're going to travel the world."

"And they're leaving the entire business to you?" Garth asked.

"Yeah."

"This calls for a celebration," Lee said, raising his beer. "To bringing the firm into the twenty-first century."

They all laughed.

"Damn, it might mean I'll have some decent competition," Garth complained. He turned to David. "Want to dump your old man and join me?"

"Actually, I'll be acting CEO as of next month." He chuckled at the absolute shock on his friends' faces.

"Your dad's retiring?" Garth asked.

"He's going into politics."

"Shit, that can't be good," Colin said.

David frowned. "What do you mean?"

Colin exchanged a glance with Lee. "Your father's not known for his political correctness."

David laughed. "Sure, he's conservative, and he can be stubborn at times, but he's always got the good of the company on his mind."

Lee shook his head. "Maybe so, but politics isn't Dionysus. He can't get away with that stuff in the public arena."

David frowned.

"Lee's right," Garth said. "Bob going into politics isn't going to be good for anyone, unless they're white and rich."

"You think so?"

"Of course," Colin said. Lee nodded.

David took a handful of chips and ate them. Were they

right? The conversation with Bob on Monday came to mind. Would his father be blind to the immigrants' fate after David showed him the facts? No, his father always listened to him. Plus, he had more information to sway him. David had spoken to all of Zita's foster sisters the other night, and had added their stories to his file.

"Anyone else got work-related news they want to share?" Lee asked. "'Cause I've got news of a different nature."

"What's up?" Colin asked.

"We're having a girl." He grinned and pulled a photo out of his jacket pocket, dropping it on the table in front of them.

"You poor bastard," Garth said. "She's going to have you wrapped around her little finger."

"I know." Lee was beaming.

David put his concern aside and picked up the ultrasound picture. It didn't look human to him, but he wasn't going to say so.

"You going to paint the nursery pink?" Colin cringed.

"Hell no. She's not having any of that gender defining stuff. She can choose to play with trucks and cars, or dolls, or both. Whatever she wants, she's going to have."

The baby was one lucky kid. "Congratulations." David raised his wine glass and they toasted Lee's unborn child.

"All right guys, let's play some poker," Lee said when they were done. "I need more money to buy my baby girl a monster truck."

Amid laughter, David dealt the cards.

Sometime later, the pizza arrived. They halted the game while they grabbed slices and stood around the kitchen eating.

"Nice bowl," Colin commented, picking up the fruit bowl David had bought in the flea market. "Where'd you get it?"

"Flea market at Discovery Green."

The three of them stared at him.

"What were you doing at a flea market?" Garth asked.

He wasn't sure why they were so surprised. "I was on a date."

Lee laughed. "I can't imagine one of your socialites at a flea market."

"She's not a socialite," David said, refusing to get riled.

"Sounds intriguing." Garth waggled his eyebrows. "Tell us more. Where did you meet?"

"She's the sister of a friend." He was kind of reluctant to tell them about Zita. He wanted to keep the relationship to himself until he'd figured out where it was going.

"What friend? We're your friends." Colin was indignant.

"Carolina Flanagan."

Garth whistled. "Now that's someone in your league."

David laughed.

"Has your dad met her?" Colin asked at the same time as Lee said, "What's her name?"

"Zita. She met Dad at a refugee symposium before we were dating."

Colin winced. "How did it go?"

David grinned at the memory. "She called him a racist bigot and walked away." He wished he had a camera to take a picture of their faces.

"I have got to meet this woman," Lee said.

The others nodded.

"So are you still dating her?" Colin asked.

"Yeah. She's one of a kind."

Lee nudged Garth. "He's got it bad."

"He sure does."

"Got what?" David asked.

"The lurve bug," Lee told him. "Your face went all sappy just now."

David frowned. It was too soon to consider love.

"What does your father think about that?" Colin asked.

"He doesn't know I'm dating her. I haven't introduced them yet."

"Good idea," Lee said. "Get the ring on her finger before she meets your family."

"Hold up there." David's heart raced as he backed up. "No one's talking about rings. Besides, she's already met Dad."

"Give it up, guys," Garth said. "They'll be fine. Let's get back to playing cards."

David shot his friend a grateful glance.

His heart told him they would be fine, but after what Colin

had said, his head wasn't so sure. Perhaps it was time to introduce Zita to his family, if only to prove them wrong. He was sure his mother would like Zita, and Bob would forgive her for the bigot comment as soon as he spoke with her.

David would arrange something soon.

Chapter 11

On Saturday morning, Zita woke early. David was picking her up, and after they'd taken the dogs for a walk, they were going to do something together, just the two of them. Walking into the kitchen, she found Beatriz holding Xaviera, and Alejandra feeding Julio.

"*Buenos días*," she said, heading for the coffee machine.

"Morning," the girls replied.

"Where's Mama?"

Alejandra nodded to the back door. "In the garden, of course."

"Have you had breakfast?" Zita asked, putting some bread in the toaster.

The girls shook their head.

"What do you want?" She was happy to get the girls some food while they held the two babies, who were blissfully quiet at the moment.

When Zita was done, she took Xaviera from Beatriz so she could eat, and wandered outside to find her mother.

Carmen was weeding her vegetable beds.

"*Hola, Mamá.*"

"*Niñita*, how are you today?"

"I'm feeling well, thanks."

Carmen examined her carefully and then nodded as if satisfied. "Good, you've been looking very tired lately."

"We all have. It's hard work with the babies." Though her mother never appeared tired. Nothing seemed to faze her.

"*Sí*. Have you plans for the day?"

"I'm taking the dogs for a walk with David."

Her mother smiled. "You are seeing a bit of David. He's a nice man."

"He is," Zita agreed.

Xaviera started fretting. Zita shushed her, jiggling her up and down gently.

"Is Elena up yet?" Carmen asked.

"I haven't seen her. Beatriz had Xaviera when I came downstairs."

Carmen frowned.

Zita understood why. Elena was struggling to cope with motherhood. At only fourteen, she hadn't wanted to have the baby, but by the time she'd arrived in the States she'd had no choice. "Do you think it's post-partum depression?"

Carmen shook her head. "No. We will keep an eye on her though. It might be best to offer Xaviera up for adoption."

Zita held the baby closer, sheltering her. It was a practical solution, but her heart felt the warmth of the baby girl against her chest and she didn't want to be parted from her. "Elena may still change her mind."

Her mother sighed. "It is too late to stop either of us getting attached." She ran a hand over Xaviera's hair. "But it might be the best for the baby."

Carmen was right. Xaviera wriggled and put her hand in her mouth. "I'll take her inside and see that she's fed."

Slowly she walked back into the house. Julio was in his portable crib and Beatriz and Alejandra were watching music videos on the television. "Is Elena in her room?"

Bea nodded. "She's sleeping."

She would have to wake up to feed Xaviera. Zita headed upstairs and knocked on Elena's door. When there was no answer, she pushed it open and found her sprawled across her bed asleep.

"Elena, wake up. Xaviera needs feeding."

As if to punctuate the point, Xaviera started wailing.

Elena sat up slowly, brushing her hair out of her face. "Give her here," she said with a scowl.

Zita handed the baby over and Elena fed her. Perhaps it would be better if they switched Xaviera over to formula. Then any of them could feed her, but it may also keep Elena from bonding with the girl. Zita wasn't sure what to do. She couldn't blame Elena for not wanting the child. She was so young, and she'd been raped.

When the baby was fed Zita took her and Elena turned over to go back to sleep. Zita sighed, gathered a new diaper and some clothes for Xaviera, and left the room. She'd use Alejandra's room to wash the baby and get her ready for the day.

By the time she was done, David was due to arrive. She gave Xaviera to Carmen and packed a day pack for herself. As she was finishing, Bess and Saint started barking. She grabbed her things and headed for the front door. "I'm off, Mama. Call me if you need anything."

"Have fun."

She opened the door as David was about to knock. He was carrying his own backpack and dressed in jeans, blue T-shirt and tennis shoes.

"Hi," she said and kissed him quickly. "Let's go. If you come in, we won't get out again for at least half an hour."

He grinned and followed her to her SUV, opening the back so the dogs could get in.

"Where are we going?" David asked as she drove out of the yard.

"There's a place not too far from here that's nice and the dogs can roam off the leash."

"Sounds good. So is Casa Flanagan the madhouse that it was last weekend?"

"Not yet. Most of the girls aren't up."

"So why the rush?"

His question made her think. She'd been in a hurry to get out of the house, wanting to escape. "It's Elena."

David waited for her to continue.

"She's not handling motherhood very well. I know it's only been two weeks, but she wants as little to do with Xaviera as possible."

"How come?"

"It could be many reasons." She shrugged. "Fourteen is so young to be having a baby." She was hardly more than a child herself.

Zita pulled into the parking lot and turned off the engine. After letting the dogs out and grabbing her backpack, she joined David on the path.

"Let's go this way." She pointed, whistled for her dogs to come, and started down the path.

David took hold of her hand and the simple gesture comforted her.

"It must be hard for her," he said. "New country, new baby, not sure whether she'll be allowed to stay. I imagine her emotions are all over the place."

"She's arguing with everyone, even Beatriz. They had such a fight when Bea was allowed to stay in the country."

"Why?"

"Elena's scared she'll be sent back. It's an odd issue, because Xaviera is a US citizen. That might work in Elena's favor, but there have been cases where a parent has been deported even if their child is a citizen. We've not been able to get much proof of her abuse."

"Except Xaviera."

Zita nodded. "But it's her word that she was raped, which might not be enough."

Bess trotted up to her, her expression hopeful. Zita reached into the backpack and drew out the ball. Bess jumped around in delight and then sped after the ball when Zita threw it.

"Sometimes I think life would be so much nicer if I were a dog," she said.

"Only if you had a kind owner."

She sighed. "True." She had to cheer up. She wasn't being a very pleasant date. "So how was your poker night?"

"Great. Colin's parents are retiring, so he's taking over the family business, and Lee showed us an ultrasound of his baby girl. He's going to be wrapped around her finger."

Zita smiled. "He's looking forward to being a daddy?"

"Absolutely. He's more excited than his wife. He's been reading all the baby books and taking notes for the nursery."

"That's great. What about your other friend, Garth wasn't

it?"

"Yeah. He's fine." David was silent for a moment, then opened his mouth as if to speak and closed it again.

"What's wrong?"

He sighed. "Just something the guys said about Dad."

Curious, she asked, "What did they say?"

"That he wasn't right for politics."

She glanced at him. He seemed uncertain. "What do you think?"

"Dad's always been Dad. Sure, he can be a bit aggressive at times, and he's conservative, but he has to show he's in control."

"You never thought he was over the top?"

"Well, yes, but that's just who he is."

"And will who he is be good in politics?"

"I don't know." He ran a hand through his hair. "Part of me wants to say no just because I don't want to be CEO."

Zita hesitated. "Have you told him that?"

"No. I've only just realized it myself." He shook his head. "How can I tell him? I've been groomed for the position since I was young and he wants to move on. It's hardly fair."

"You need to be happy as well." She glanced over to him. "Do you know what you'd do instead?"

"Set up my own business."

His response was so quick, he'd obviously been thinking about. "Doing what?"

"Consulting, helping other businesses grow."

She smiled. "That sounds like a great idea."

He shrugged. "It's too late now."

"It's never too late. You just need to set some goals."

He looked at her and raised an eyebrow. "Where have I heard that before?"

"This really smart guy told me about it." She squeezed his hand.

"That guy didn't think it would apply to himself."

"Why don't you ask your siblings if they want to take over Dionysus?" Zita asked.

"There's not enough time to get them up to speed."

"So you stay as acting CEO until they are. You can always

plan your business at the same time."

David sighed. "Yeah, I guess."

She hugged him. "We can set some goals this afternoon."

He smiled. "All right."

Bess ran over and looked up at Zita expectantly.

"These two need a run," she said. "It won't take them long to tire out, and then we can find somewhere to have the sandwiches I brought."

"I'm not much of a runner."

"That's fine. I'll take them for a loop around the park and meet you on the other side."

Saint ran over, his coat wet and muddy. Zita jumped in front of David, shepherding Saint away. Saint bounded next to her and shook himself, mud and water flicking all over her. She groaned. Of course her dogs would find the only puddle on the field. She was covered in mud splatters.

David winced. "Thanks for taking the hit. You're my hero." He pulled her close and kissed her slowly.

She smiled against his lips as she ran her hands down his back to his butt and squeezed. Then she drew back. Now was not the time to get frisky, especially with the dogs around. "No problem. I won't be long."

"See you on the other side."

Zita set off, stopping every now and then to throw the ball for her dogs. Halfway across the field her foot slipped and she flailed to regain her footing. Bess thought she was playing a game and jumped around her. Zita leaned back to avoid stepping on her, landing with a plop on her butt. She swore as the water seeped into her pants.

Saint raced over with the ball in his mouth. He dropped it at Zita's feet and the two dogs rolled in the mud.

She groaned. It was too late to stop them.

Zita grabbed the ball and carefully got to her feet. She brushed ineffectually at the mud on her butt and legs. She was filthy, and there was nothing she could do about it.

After the dogs had had their fill of the mud bath, she kept them busy throwing the ball, while she watched David on the far side of the field. He had his phone out and it looked as though he was taking photos.

He was an interesting combination. When she'd first met him, she'd taken him for a rich boy, not sure if his interest in learning more about her foster sisters was genuine. But he'd really captured her heart when he'd volunteered to help out last weekend. To stay and put up with all the crazy that was her household showed a great deal of fortitude.

He was a lot like her, going with the family expectations so he didn't let anyone down. She wanted to help him.

She made her way across the field, and her dogs barked and played together, having a fabulous time. She grinned at their antics, relaxing a little.

When she reached David, she called her dogs to her side, putting them on their leashes. "How's it going?"

"Great." He turned to her and his eyes widened. "What happened to you?" His mouth twitched.

"I found a mud pit." She wanted to take her shoes off and squeeze the water out of her socks.

"Ah." He grinned then. "Those towels in your car are going to come in handy again."

She rolled her eyes. "Are you hungry?"

"Yeah."

Zita looked for a good place to sit. Brushing the dirt off her hands as much as she could, she then got the picnic blanket out of her backpack and spread it on the ground for David. She settled her dogs with water and a chew treat at a distance so they didn't dirty him, and used some of the water to wash her hands. "Have a seat."

"You've come organized," David commented as she handed him a sandwich.

"I figured if the weather stayed clear, it would be nice to spend a bit longer out here. Bess and Saint don't get the chance to run during the week."

"What about you?"

"Me?" She frowned at him. "I don't need to run."

"I meant you don't get the chance to be alone."

She shrugged. "It is what it is."

"How's the study going?"

Zita brushed her hair off her face. "Not great." She was beginning to think she should skip the test and do it later in the year.

"You could come over to my place this afternoon to study."

She hoped study was a euphemism. She wanted an afternoon free of responsibility. "I'd like that." Spotting David's phone, she asked, "Did you take some photos?"

"Yeah." He handed his phone over.

It was interesting to see what captured his attention. There were closeups of tree bark and flowers, shots of clumps of trees, and then landscapes of the entire field. She and the dogs appeared in one, and she looked sad.

"What were you thinking about?" David asked, looking over her shoulder at the photos.

"Life." It sounded so stupid.

He wrapped an arm around her shoulders and pulled her close. She leaned into him, enjoying the support and comfort he offered.

"Hearing the foster girls' stories puts my life into perspective," David said. "I've never had anything but first-world problems."

"They can be important."

He shook his head. "Not like what you deal with."

Zita didn't know what to say.

The sun disappeared behind the clouds and the day turned dark.

"We should head back," David said.

Zita nodded. She took the hand he offered and let him pull her to her feet.

Chapter 12

When they arrived back at Casa Flanagan, David was pleased the house was quiet. He'd half expected a new crisis that would prevent Zita from getting away for the afternoon.

They took the dogs out the back to wash. He held the hose while Zita rubbed her dogs clean. She looked so cute with her butt covered in mud that he couldn't resist. He directed the spray at her pants.

She squealed and whirled to face him.

"Sorry." He grinned. "Thought you'd like to get clean too."

She narrowed her eyes and took a step toward him as Bess shook the water from her coat, covering Zita. She laughed and slumped in mock defeat. "You might have a point."

When the dogs were clean and towel-dried, Zita and David headed inside. Carmen was in the kitchen, stirring a pot and holding one of the babies.

"Did you have a nice walk?" she asked.

"It was a bit grubby," Zita said. "I'm going to take a shower, but I wanted to check you still don't need me this afternoon."

"No. Everything is under control." Carmen smiled. "You go and have fun. Will you be home for lunch tomorrow?"

"Of course." Zita turned to David. "Do you want to come to lunch? Carly and Bridget will be here."

His heart jumped. She was inviting him to the family lunch. "Sure."

"Great. Let me get cleaned up and then we'll head to your place."

He tagged her arm as she walked past and murmured to her, "You could pack an overnight bag if you want."

She kissed him quickly. "Will do." She flashed a look at her mother and grinned. "Won't be long."

Left alone with Carmen, David wasn't entirely sure what to say. They hadn't spoken one-on-one before.

The baby in Carmen's arms grizzled. Carmen sighed. "Hush now, Xaviera." She swayed with her.

"Do you want me to take her?" David asked. After he'd gotten used to the baby last weekend, it had been nice holding her. And the practice would come in handy for Lee's baby.

"That would be great."

Carmen passed the baby over and David carefully cradled Xaviera's head, shushing her and kissing her soft downy hair. His chest swelled. She was so young and innocent, and yet her creation had been one of violence. "Where's Elena?"

Carmen sighed. "Out in the garden with Beatriz. I thought it would do her good to get some fresh air."

He wanted to ask whether Carmen thought Elena would keep Xaviera, but it was none of his business. He kept rocking the baby, singing her a lullaby he remembered from his childhood, and she eventually quieted.

"You're good with babies," Carmen commented.

"Beginner's luck," he said, slightly uncomfortable with the way she was examining him.

"Some people are naturals." She smiled.

He glanced down at Xaviera who was now sleeping. Perhaps he'd picked up some of his mother's talents. He sat down on one of the stools and pressed another kiss against Xaviera's head. She smelled like talcum powder.

"How's Teresa's case coming along?" He hadn't asked Zita about it, had wanted to give her a break.

"Johanna has filled in the necessary paperwork to claim asylum, which means Teresa's case is now stronger."

"Zita mentioned that."

Carmen looked toward the living room where the television was on and lowered her voice. "Johanna took quite a risk.

Fernando said it took several hours, and she was bound to have been missed. I hope she came up with a reasonable excuse."

David hoped so too.

Zita walked in carrying an overnight bag and looking delectable. Her hair was tied back in a ponytail and she wore plaid leggings and an oversized sweater that hung off one shoulder. Her face softened when she saw him. "You're getting cuddle time."

"Yes. Carmen says I'm a natural."

Zita raised an eyebrow. "I suspect she's right."

He wasn't so sure, but it was kind of nice holding Xaviera.

"Shall we get going, or do you want to snuggle some more?" Zita asked.

He'd rather snuggle time with Zita. "We can go." He got to his feet. "Where should I put Xaviera?"

"You can take her with you if you like," Carmen said.

David stiffened and both women laughed.

"I'll grab the rocker." Zita left the room and returned moments later with it.

David carefully placed the baby in and gave her a kiss. "See you next time." When he stood up, Zita was watching him with a strange expression on her face. "What's wrong?"

She shook her head. "Nothing. Let's go."

He said goodbye to Carmen and followed Zita outside to his car.

By the time they reached his apartment, the rain had set in. He made them both hot drinks and they settled on the couch.

"Do you want help studying for the test?"

"There's nothing you can do. It's mostly reading and comprehension." She sighed. "I don't know why I'm bothering."

"You still want to be a lawyer, don't you?"

"Yeah. I'm just tired." She lowered her eyes. "Though there might be something that will wake me up." The look she gave him was full of suggestion and parts of his anatomy twitched awake.

He was tempted to draw her into his arms and follow through on her suggestion, but he knew how much the test meant to her. He shifted away. "You want a reward before you've done the work," he teased. "You're going to have to wait."

She pouted. "I bet I can make it worth your while."

She was a temptress. "I'm sure you can." He stood, gathered both mugs and moved to the kitchen to resist her. "Why don't you get your laptop out?"

Her loud huff made him smile. "What are you going to do?" she asked.

He returned to the living room where she was rummaging in her bag. "I can read a book."

"Ooh, what are you reading?" She switched on her computer.

"We can talk about that later too." He didn't want to give her any excuse to procrastinate.

"Fine." She curled up on the sofa. "You know, maybe you should write down your business goals."

His chest tightened. "Maybe."

She gave him a no-nonsense look.

"All right." It was a pointless exercise, he'd never go through with it, but it would keep Zita happy.

"Great." She started typing.

David got up and grabbed a notebook and then sat next to her, but didn't start writing. He was content just to watch her, see the little furrow between her eyebrows as she worked and the way she bit her lip when she was concentrating. She was completely engrossed in what she was doing.

"Would you stop staring at me? It's making me self-conscious." She didn't look up.

He grinned. OK, so maybe she wasn't completely engrossed. "Just enjoying the view."

She snorted.

With a smile, he got to work.

***

"I am so done," Zita declared some time later, closing her laptop and rubbing her eyes. She wasn't sure how long she'd been studying, but she couldn't take in another thing.

David looked up. "Are you hungry?"

"Yes." But she was hungry for more than food. She placed her laptop on the coffee table. They hadn't had much time in private since they'd started dating, and now that she'd done her homework, she wanted to make full use of their seclusion. "But first, it's time for my reward."

His answering grin sent heat right through her, blasting through her fatigue. He was so damn sexy. She shuffled along the couch and straddled him. Then she lowered her head until her lips were almost touching his and paused, enjoying the anticipation. His breath was warm and he watched her, waiting. With a smile she pressed her lips to his. Her heart sighed as she deepened the kiss, tasting the hot chocolate he'd had earlier.

His arms wrapped around her, pulling her closer. A feeling of security swept over Zita and as he cupped her butt, her arousal shot into overdrive. She wanted him now. Breaking the kiss, she ripped off her sweater and reached for her bra strap.

"Wait." David's hands stopped her from unclasping her bra. "Slow down." He kissed her chin, her neck, down to her shoulder . . . slow, tender kisses.

She dropped her hands and reached for him, letting her head fall to the side as he found a spot on her neck that made her moan.

"You're so beautiful, Zita. I want to savor you." His hands brushed her breasts, his thumbs caressing her nipples, and her whole body was alive with sensations.

Gently he brought her face to his and his kiss intoxicated her, slowly and luxuriously.

"I need you in my bed." Before she could move, he'd lifted her up and she wrapped her legs around his waist as he carried her into the bedroom, and then lowered her on to the mattress. He rid himself of his clothes and then climbed over her. His hand brushed her cheek as he kissed her again, and Zita's heart filled.

She loved him.

She loved his tenderness, his sensitivity, his hands. Seeing him today with Xaviera had touched her deeply and now, with the care he was showing her, it tipped into love.

She gasped as he caressed her breasts and his mouth followed the path that they took.

Slowly, he dragged her leggings from her, kissing down her thighs, desperately close to the heat pooling in her groin. Zita shifted, thrusting her hips, trying to tempt him.

He chuckled softly. "Patience, my love."

The words pierced a hole right through her heart. Did he mean them?

He threw her leggings to the floor and slowly crawled his way back up to her, stopping only to press a kiss against her panties.

"David," she gasped.

His lips brushed hers and he kissed her slowly. She wrapped her legs around him, needing to be closer, and poured all of her love into the kiss.

"Zita." The reverent way he said her name sent her head spinning. He unclasped her bra, peeled it off and then took one of her breasts in his mouth.

She was on sensation overload as he turned his attention to the other breast. Zita wasn't used to this slow and sensual way of lovemaking. She wasn't sure she'd be able to handle much more. She wanted him, all of him.

He moved lower, hovering over her groin as he glanced up, teasing her.

"Take them off," she said, pushing at her underpants.

"Always in such a rush." He brushed her hands away and put his mouth to the cotton. It wasn't enough. She squirmed to have more, thrusting her hips upward.

David groaned and dragged her underwear away. Then finally he pressed his mouth to her crotch.

Zita jerked as pleasure flooded her. At the rate she was going, she wasn't going to last very long.

His tongue swirled, making her moan, before he stopped and moved back up her body, kissing his way up.

"David." She couldn't help the complaint in her voice.

"You're so amazing," he said, kissing her neck. "I need to taste all of you."

"Where you were was just fine." She gasped as he nibbled a sensitive spot at the base of her neck.

"All in good time."

She wasn't able to sway him. Her body throbbed and sang as

he kissed and licked his way over her breasts, down her stomach and to her core. Every touch, every movement, made her body twitch in need.

"Please, David."

"If you insist."

She almost cried out in thanks as he grabbed a condom and sheathed himself. Then he slid ever so slowly into her, kissing her lips with such passion as he did.

Zita moved with him, overwhelmed by feelings, sensations. Pressure built and his movements became faster until she shattered as she came. All she heard was David calling her name.

She was lost.

It took some time before Zita's brain began to function again. David had cleaned up and rejoined her on the bed, pulling her close to him.

"Are you all right?"

Tears pricked her eyes and she was glad he was behind her, spooning her. She nodded. "Of course." But she wasn't. How could she be, now she realized how much she loved him? It was terrifying and exciting. No one had ever made her feel so worshiped. She pulled his arm around her and clasped his hand against her chest. She wanted to tell him how she felt, but it was too soon. He'd freak out.

"Are you hungry?"

She swallowed and let out a deep breath. "A little."

He kissed her shoulder and then her neck and said quietly into her ear, "What would you like?"

"Anything, as long as I don't have to go out."

He hummed in agreement. "Tonight is the perfect night for staying in bed. There's a Mexican place that delivers."

"Sounds great." She turned over and hugged him fiercely, needing to be closer to him.

He smiled as she drew back. "What was that for?"

"For giving me the best sex of my life." She said it playfully, hoping to lighten her own mood.

His grin was huge. "Well now, I'm glad to satisfy."

"You did." She kissed him quickly and then sat up on the

edge of the bed. "Let's get some food." She grabbed her clothes and wandered out of the bedroom to give herself more time to control her emotions.

Now she had found him, she didn't want to let him go.

But did he feel the same about her?

***

Last night had been amazing. David had explored Zita's body and discovered what really aroused her. She was so wonderfully responsive and made him feel like a sex god. He stretched and then pulled Zita closer for a snuggle. She mumbled in her sleep, but didn't wake up. He smiled, kissing her neck.

Checking the time, he carefully got out of bed so as not to disturb her. He'd make them both breakfast before they headed to Casa Flanagan for lunch.

In the kitchen, he scrambled up a couple of eggs and made the coffee. Then he carried the breakfast tray back into his bedroom and placed it on the bedside table.

Zita was sprawled out over the mattress, the sheets exposing the tops of her breasts. "Time to wake up, beautiful." He ran a hand gently over her hair and pressed a kiss against her brow.

"Mmhuf," she muttered, turning away from him.

He lay down on the bed next to her. He nibbled on her neck and caressed her breasts, enjoying the way she unconsciously pressed herself toward him. "I made you breakfast," he murmured. "And if you wake up now, we might have time for other things before we go to lunch." He ran his hand under the sheets, along her side and between her legs.

Zita moaned. "We definitely have time for that." Her eyes opened and she turned onto her back, reaching for him. "Come here."

The demand shot straight to his groin.

Breakfast could wait.

"I could get used to waking up like that each day," Zita said when they were done.

"I agree." His heart raced at his words. He could definitely get used to waking up next to Zita, and that was kind of scary. He brushed a kiss on her lips and then handed her the cup of coffee, which was still warm. "Though next time I'll wake you up before I make breakfast."

"I'm not complaining." She took a sip and grinned at him.

"I'll reheat the eggs." He grabbed the plate and hurried away.

A quick examination of the food had him tossing it in the trash and starting a new batch.

The fact he liked Zita was clear. She was interesting, kind, and fun to be around. There was no denying he was attracted to her, but should he be having long-term thoughts about her?

All of a sudden, the comments his friends had made about Bob came rushing back. He'd never thought ethnicity was a problem, but now . . . he wasn't as certain as he'd like to be. If he was lucky, Bob wouldn't remember Zita at all.

She wandered out naked and he lost his train of thought. She was beautiful.

"Any of those eggs for me?" she asked.

"Of course." He dished up and handed her a plate.

He'd think about it later.

***

They were first to arrive at Casa Flanagan. Inside, both babies were screaming, and voices were raised. Zita winced as she hurried through the door, not waiting for him.

David followed at a slower pace, to let Zita find out what was going on.

In the living room, Alejandra and Elena were shouting at each other, both holding crying babies in their arms. Carmen was standing in the middle trying to calm them, but everything was in Spanish so David had no idea what was going on. Zita took Xaviera from Elena and passed her to David. "Take her for me."

Surprised, he hugged the baby against his chest, whispering nonsensical words to her. He had to get her away from the noise and tension in the room. He gestured to Zita that he was heading for the kitchen.

"Hush now, sweetheart," he said, kissing Xaviera on the head. "It's all right."

The baby's cries immediately lessened, and by the time Zita carried a crying Julio in, Xaviera was quiet.

131

"The baby whisperer," Zita said with a smile as she shushed Julio.

Xaviera gurgled and when he glanced down at her, she smiled at him. The tug on his heart was painful. "What's going on in there?"

Zita sighed. "Alejandra is accusing Elena of being a bad mother, of acting like a child."

The evidence of how well that had gone down could still be heard in the living room.

"She *is* still a child," he pointed out.

"I know. Mama's going to talk to her about adoption again."

David's arms tightened involuntarily around Xaviera.

New voices could be heard at the front door.

"Carly and Evan have arrived," Zita said.

Moments later they walked into the kitchen. Carly's eyebrows rose at David holding the baby. "*Hola.*" She kissed his cheeks and then kissed the baby's head. "I didn't expect you to be so cozy with Xaviera."

"I'm getting better," David said, adjusting the baby so he could shake Evan's hand.

"He's a baby whisperer," Zita told them. "Xaviera stops crying whenever he holds her."

"Must be his calm nature," Carly said.

David didn't say a word.

Teresa hurried into the kitchen holding a notebook. She hesitated when she saw David. He smiled at her, hoping to put her at ease.

"Hey, Teresa!" Evan said. "Are they your new drawings?"

She nodded.

"I'd love to see them. Shall we go into the dining room?"

She nodded again and followed Evan out of the room.

Zita waited until they were gone before she said, "Evan's the only man she's really comfortable with."

"Yes," Carly said. "They bonded over art and Evan says she's very good. He was talking about arranging an exhibition for her if she gets to stay."

"The hearing's next week?" David asked.

"Yeah, next Wednesday," Zita said.

He'd arranged to get the time off work so he could see the

whole process through. He was already firmly in favor of letting all of the girls stay.

Bridget and Jack entered the kitchen. "What's for lunch?" Bridget asked, grabbing a piece of fruit from the bench.

"Good question." Zita handed Julio to Carly and checked the fridge, dragging things out.

"Where is everyone?" Jack asked.

"Hiding," Zita said, and explained about the argument that had now gone quiet in the living room.

Carmen walked in, sighing. "*Hola, mis bebes.*" She hugged her daughters and Jack, and then hugged David, being careful of Xaviera.

Warmth spread through David's body. She was treating him like one of the family.

Carmen glanced over to where Zita was putting together something for lunch. "Let's order pizza."

The three sisters looked at each other, their eyes wide. This was obviously not a regular occurrence.

"Are you all right, Mama?" Carly asked.

"I am tired today, and we could all do with a treat." She brushed a stray hair out of her face. "Why don't you order, and I'll pick some mint from the garden for a drink." She headed outside.

"That's odd behavior, right?" Jack asked.

Bridget nodded. "Mama believes store-bought pizza is awful."

"The situation with Elena is getting to her," Zita said, and quickly explained how Elena wasn't coping with becoming a mother. "Do you want to order, and I'll go and talk to her?"

"Let's all go," Bridget said. "Jack, you can handle the food, right?"

He nodded.

The girls walked outside and David was left holding the baby. He wasn't quite sure what to say to Jack. He didn't know him very well, even though Jack worked at one of Dionysus' plants.

"Which baby have you got there?" Jack asked as he picked up the computer tablet and typed.

"Xaviera." He should know that. Julio was much bigger than

Xaviera. David blinked as annoyance welled up in him. That was weird.

"I thought so. Have you got a preference for toppings?"

"No." He took a seat. Xaviera was now sleeping.

Jack ordered and then asked David, "Have you got used to Casa Flanagan yet?" His smile was friendly.

David chuckled. "Almost. It's a lot more vibrant than what I'm used to."

Jack nodded. "Vibrant is a good word. Carmen is amazing and all the girls have thrived under her."

"It's pretty incredible what she and Zita do." Xaviera was getting heavy, so he shifted her to his other shoulder. "Is the stroller in the laundry?"

Jack left the room, and was back moments later with the folded stroller. Both of them looked at it. "There must be a button somewhere," Jack said.

At that moment, Beatriz walked in.

"Beatriz, can you set up the stroller for us?" David asked.

She smiled shyly at the two men and nodded. In seconds, she'd unfolded the stroller and locked it into the upright position.

"Thanks," he said. "I'll have to get you to show me how to do it one day." He placed Xaviera inside and covered her with a blanket.

"Is lunch almost ready?" Beatriz asked.

"We're in charge, so we're getting pizza," Jack said.

Beatriz giggled. "I'll tell the others."

Remembering the news, David turned to Jack. "I forgot to congratulate you on getting engaged."

"Thanks. I'm so glad it didn't take Bridge long to ask. I was itching to put a ring on her finger."

"You didn't ask her?"

"No. She wanted to take things slowly, because I was her boss. When she realized she loved me, she wanted to take time to enjoy it and not rush."

David understood. Things were moving fast for him and Zita as well, and her family had accepted him without a second thought.

Would she get the same reception from his family? The idea

that his friends might be right didn't sit well with him, but he had to consider it. Would Bob alienate Zita?

Because that wouldn't be OK at all.

Chapter 13

Carmen wasn't out at the mint patch.

"She'll be by Papa's tree," Zita said. They walked through the garden, and found her sitting under a tree that had been planted in honor of their father. Tears were running down her face.

"Mama," Zita said and hurried to hug her.

"*Niñitas.*" She sniffed and wiped her eyes. "Do not worry. I am all right."

"No you're not, Mama," Bridget said. "What's wrong?"

She and Carly sat either side of her, Carly still holding Julio.

Carmen sighed. "It has been a little bit difficult the past few weeks," she said. "I don't know what I would have done without Zita's help." She patted Zita's knee and smiled at her.

The stab of guilt made it hard to breathe. This was why she couldn't leave. Her mother needed her.

"What can we do to help?" Carly asked.

"Nothing. It will work itself out in the end. Elena is scared of being sent home, so she won't consider giving Xaviera up for adoption, though she doesn't want the child. She believes that because the baby is a US citizen, she will be allowed to stay as well, but if she gives her up, she will have to go home."

"When is her hearing?" Bridget asked.

"Next month," Zita answered.

"Then there's Teresa," Carmen continued. "She asks for

news on her mother and sister every day."

Zita winced. The girl's concern was understandable, but the process was slow.

"We'll buy the airfares as soon as the application is approved," Carly said.

"It won't be that easy," Carmen said. "Johanna is being monitored all of the time and Manuela is rarely permitted to visit her family. Getting them away is going to be difficult."

"Why didn't you tell me that?" Zita asked. She'd heard nothing more about Teresa's family.

"You've been busy with the babies, and with David."

Her heart squeezed. So now she'd dropped the ball because she had a social life. Was it really going to be all or nothing?

"Perhaps Fernando can help," Carly suggested.

Carmen nodded. "He is trying. He's arranged a way to communicate with Johanna and given her both our numbers."

"That's great. Hopefully it will ease Teresa's mind," Bridget said.

"Yes," Carmen agreed. She sighed and got to her feet. "We should go inside and check what the boys have ordered." She grimaced.

Bridget and Carly laughed, but Zita wasn't able to. It was clear her mother needed her.

How could she pursue her dreams now?

***

Monday evening, when the house had grown silent, Zita closed herself in her bedroom. She should study for her LSAT, but after yesterday she couldn't go through with it. She couldn't abandon her mother. She'd spend the evening researching her Irish heritage instead. She flicked on her laptop and crawled onto her bed. Before she got started, there was a knock on her door.

She sighed. "Yes?"

Her mother came in. She was holding a letter.

"What's up?"

"This came for you today." She held it out and Zita took it.

The logo on the corner of the envelope made her freeze. It was the Law School Admissions Council.

Feck.

"Is there something you want to talk to me about?" Carmen didn't appear upset.

What was she supposed to say? Zita shifted her laptop onto her bedside table and sat on the edge of the bed. "It was something I was considering." She threw the envelope in the trash. "It doesn't matter, I'm not going to do it anymore."

"Why not? You would make a good lawyer."

Zita stared at her mother. "Do you think so?"

"Of course. You have the passion and determination. Why have you never said anything?"

Zita hesitated. Should she admit to her mother how unhappy she was? Should she confide all of her plans and hope she understood?

"*Niñita*, you've not been happy. Talk to me."

She stared at Carmen. "What?"

Her mother tutted. "You think I don't know when my child is upset? I've been waiting, hoping you will talk to me when you're ready."

Hell. Zita had to be truthful. She took hold of Carmen's hand. "I wanted to become an immigration lawyer. I wanted to fight for my sisters in the courtroom, not just hold their hands."

"And you no longer want to?"

"Mama, you need my help too much." Zita sighed. "The girls need so much support, I can't leave you to do it on your own, and studying law would take up so many hours."

"*Pfft.* What nonsense is this?"

Zita sat back.

"Three of the girls are at school full-time. The other three need help, yes, but not so much that you have to give up what you want."

"But yesterday you were so upset, you said you needed me."

"Yesterday I was emotional." She waved her hand. "Sometimes it even gets on top of me, but I don't want my daughter to feel obligated. Are you happy?"

"I was . . ." That was the truth. "But now I want a little bit more." How could she explain it without making it seem like she didn't value what her mother was doing? "I feel so useless when I sit in the courtroom. With each new girl, we go through the same thing and we're not getting anywhere."

Carmen nodded. "It is endless, but we're making a difference."

"*You're* making a difference," she said. "You have all the work with the migrant community as well as the foster girls. I'm just helping out."

"If you feel that way, you should definitely find something else to do." Carmen patted her arm.

"Really?" She couldn't believe how calm her mother was being.

"Of course. I want you to be happy."

"I didn't want to disappoint you. You've been doing this for so long."

"*Sí*, and perhaps neglecting my youngest child. It was hard on you when I first began to foster. You were still at school."

"No, Mama. I always had your support."

"But not all of my time. Tell me about law school."

"There's nothing to tell. I have to do an admissions test, which is on Saturday. Even if I get a good score, I still might not get in because I haven't done an undergraduate degree."

"Is the test hard?"

She shrugged. "It seems all right. I've never been the academic one."

"Nonsense. You're as smart as Bridget and Carly."

Zita didn't bother correcting her. "We'll see."

"Zita, you have always been more interested in people than study, but that doesn't mean you're not intelligent." Carmen lifted Zita's chin.

"You don't know that. Neither of us does. None of my grades were great."

"Only because school didn't interest you. I'm sure if you study what you're passionate about, you'll be fine."

Zita smiled at her mother's confidence in her. "It's been a little difficult to find the time to study.

"Then you will have homework time with the other girls. There's no getting around it."

"All right, Mama. Thank you."

She nodded. "I'll leave you to study." Carmen hugged her. "But no more keeping secrets from your mother. If you are not happy, I want to know why and how I can fix it."

Zita smiled at the stern tone. "Yes, Mama."

Carmen kissed her cheek. "I'll see you in the morning."

Waiting until she closed the door behind her, Zita exhaled slowly. Her mother knew, there was no more hiding. Now if she failed, everyone would know. Which made her all the more determined to succeed.

***

David has his music cranked loud as he worked through the numbers, checking the details in his monthly report. A hand clasped his shoulder, the grip tight, and he knew it was his father. He took the headphones off his ears and turned around.

"Damn it, David, that's it. You can't wear those things at work." His eyes were narrowed.

David smiled. "I appreciate your concern, Bob, but I'm more productive when I wear them. It blocks out unnecessary distractions."

Bob scowled. "I'm no distraction, I'm your boss."

If he wasn't used to his father's scowls and gruff nature, Bob could actually seem intimidating. Perhaps that's how other people saw him. "Absolutely," David agreed. "I wasn't referring to you. What do you need?"

"I need your monthly report *now*."

"I'm reviewing it," he said. "I'll have it to you within the hour."

"I didn't say within the hour, I said now." His chest puffed outward and his eyes brooked no argument.

It caused David to pause. What was so important? "I'm sorry, I didn't get your message about the changed deadline."

"I didn't send any message," he growled.

"Then you'll have to wait until it's finished. There are some numbers I have to check. I'll send it straight to you when I'm done."

Bob glared at him and David met his gaze without flinching.

"Fine. I want it ASAP." Bob stalked out of the office.

David let out a deep breath. Hell. His father *was* intimidating, he'd just never recognized it before.

Maybe his friends were right. Maybe Bob wouldn't be great

in politics.

The thought made him uncomfortable, so he replaced his headphones and continued to work.

***

On Wednesday evening, Zita was too distracted to study. Teresa's hearing was the next day and she was as nervous as the girl. Knowing she wouldn't be able to sleep straight away, Zita tried to find something to keep her busy. She was too agitated to read, and wouldn't be able to concentrate on television. She glanced at the list of goals she'd stuck on her wall after her talk with Carmen on Monday. She'd been meaning to add a goal to research her Irish heritage.

Well, there was no time like the present. Research would keep her busy for an hour or two and then she'd go to sleep.

Finding a couple of Irish genealogy websites, Zita entered the details she knew: her father's name, birth date and the county where he'd lived.

It took her a while to sift through the information and apply to get his birth certificate. When she was done, she searched for Flanagans in the phone book from that county. A couple of entries came up, but she wasn't ready to cold-call yet.

Still not tired, Zita figured that stalking Flanagans on social media was another way to find some answers. She laughed when hundreds of results came up. It was going to take some time to go through the names and really, was there any point? She didn't know enough to narrow it down. Someone could be a second cousin, or a great aunt or something, but Zita would have no idea who.

As she idly scrolled through the profile pictures, a guy with strawberry-blond hair caught her eye. She stared for a long moment, not quite believing it, her heart pounding. He looked exactly like her father. She clicked on the link for Sean Flanagan's profile. He had to be related to her somehow, maybe a second cousin or something. There was too much of a resemblance for it to be a coincidence.

His profile had very little information. She examined the photo. He was about thirty, had the same blue eyes as Bridget, and the same color hair as her. Zita swallowed. Should she send him a message?

He might not even reply.

With a deep breath, she clicked the button to send him a note and stared at the flashing cursor for a long while. What should she say? *We could be related?*

After a lot of thought she decided to keep it simple.

Hi!

This is going to sound weird, but please read to the end! I've been investigating my Irish heritage, and I think we might be related. You look a lot like my father — same color hair and eyes, same surname — so maybe we're second cousins or something. My father's name is Brendan Flanagan. He left Ireland in about 1984 and went to El Salvador, where he met and married my mother, and had three kids. He died when I was three, and lately I've been curious as to where he came from and if I have any other family in Ireland. Do you recognize any of this story, or perhaps have someone you could ask? I'd love to learn more.

Anyway, hopefully this hasn't freaked you out. I'd love an answer even if you know nothing.

Thanks.

Zita Flanagan

She read through it twice. It was worth a try. She hit the submit button and let out a breath.

With that done, it was definitely time for her to go to sleep. She wanted to be alert for Teresa's hearing tomorrow.

***

David checked the time and shut down his computer. If he was going to make Teresa's hearing, he had to leave now.

"David, I need you in a meeting in five," Bob called as he walked past the office.

David grabbed his coat and keys and hurried after his father. "I can't, Bob. I'm on my way out."

"Whatever it is, cancel it. This is important." Bob entered his office and grabbed a report off his desk.

David frowned. "It's Teresa's asylum hearing. I've got to go."

"I don't care. You're needed here." The scowl on Bob's face

was ferocious.

"Sorry, Bob. I promised I'd be there."

"And *I* promised you will be in this meeting." Bob stared at him. "Call whoever it is and tell them you're required at work. You're going to be CEO. You have to be flexible." He walked out of the room without waiting for David's response.

David swore and stood where he was, undecided.

"You'd better hurry," Bob's PA said from her desk. "It looks like there's real trouble," she said in a quiet voice before getting up and following Bob.

He swore again and pulled out his phone to call Zita.

***

Zita hung up from David, frowning. He wasn't going to make it. It was disappointing, but she didn't have time to dwell on it. Teresa was biting her nails in an almost obsessive manner, and at the rate she was going she'd have no nails left by the end of the hearing. Zita took hold of one of Teresa's hands. "Stop it. I know you're worried, but try to be calm. Take some deep breaths for me."

Teresa did as she was told, but then her leg started bouncing up and down.

Zita exchanged a glance with Shelly.

"Teresa Garcia."

Teresa gasped as the clerk called her name. Zita squeezed her hand. "Come on."

The three of them entered the courtroom and took their seats. The judge read the details of the case and then asked Shelly to begin.

It was a similar format to the other hearings. The evidence was presented, Teresa told her story and a lawyer for Immigration and Customs Enforcement put his case forward.

When that was done, the judge said, "You mentioned both Teresa's mother and sister have applied for asylum."

"Yes, your honor," Shelly replied.

"Do they have evidence to support their asylum claim?"

"Yes, your honor. We've been able to gather a significant amount of information about the gangs and their treatment of both Manuela and Johanna Garcia."

The judge frowned. "Is it fair to say the evidence may have some impact on Teresa's claim?"

"Yes, your honor."

"In that case I will assess both applications together."

Zita sat there, a little stunned. Both applications were going to be decided today?

"I don't understand," Teresa whispered.

Zita glanced at Shelly for the answer. She appeared as surprised as Zita was.

"They're going to assess yours and your mama's application today," Shelly told her.

Teresa's eyes widened.

The judge continued talking. She went through all of the paperwork, asked Teresa questions, and then spent some time deliberating.

"It is my judgment that the asylum and refugee applications for Teresa, Manuela and Johanna Garcia be approved."

The tension evaporated and Zita shouted, "Yes!" Her chest swelled with emotion.

Teresa tugged on her sleeve. "I get to stay?"

Zita nodded. "And your mama and sister get to come as well."

Teresa burst into tears and hugged Zita. "*Gracias, gracias.*"

"You're welcome." She held the girl tightly as the relief swept over her.

"We need to move so the next case can come in," Shelly told them with a gentle smile.

Zita helped Teresa to her feet, almost carrying her out of the room. It was the best outcome they could have asked for.

They'd saved another girl.

Chapter 14

On Sunday morning, Zita would have been perfectly happy to spend the day in bed. The excitement of Teresa's hearing and the stress from doing her LSAT yesterday had caught up with her and she wanted to pull up the covers and let David help her forget about the world. But that wasn't an option. Instead, she had to meet David's mother and sister.

"Are you ready?" David asked.

No. Zita's stomach clenched. She shouldn't be nervous. She was good with people, but this was important, this was David's family. What if they were like Bob and didn't like immigrants? Anyone who'd lived with Bob Randall for so long had to agree with his political views, didn't they? David's mother would probably take one look at her and decide she was no good for her son.

Zita checked her appearance once more and then nodded, following him out of his apartment and down to his car.

On the drive to the hotel, David said, "I'm so sorry I missed the hearing and the celebration. Teresa must be so excited. When's her family going to arrive?"

Zita pushed her worries aside. "Fernando spoke to Johanna yesterday. Manuela's birthday is coming up in a couple of weeks and the gang have given permission for her to go home and celebrate with her parents. That's going to be our best chance to get them both out."

"So what will happen?"

"I don't know yet. Carly's booked flights for that evening, but the gang might not let Manuela and Johanna celebrate alone. I'm guessing because Teresa escaped, they'll keep a close guard, so we'll have to plan it carefully."

David glanced at her. "Don't you mean Fernando will be planning it?"

"Yes, but we're offering suggestions and can provide finance if it's needed." As much as she'd like to go to El Salvador and help Teresa's family escape, she realized it was far too dangerous, and not necessary. Fernando had the expertise and knew the area.

They pulled up at a hotel that screamed first class, from its suited valet waiting patiently to take David's car keys, to the doorman waiting at the entrance. The driveway was framed with huge ornate pillars. Suddenly, Zita remembered why they were here. She was meeting David's family.

Nerves stormed her stomach and she laid a hand over her belly to settle them. The valet opened her car door and Zita forced herself to get out. She thanked the man and waited for David to give him the keys.

David smiled at her and took her hand. "Ready?"

She nodded, though she didn't think she was. "You do high tea every month?"

"Yeah. Mom loves it, and Lorelei comes when she can."

As they walked into the restaurant, the maître d' walked up to them. "Welcome Mr. Randall. Your table is over here."

Wow. They knew David by sight.

The table they were led to already had two occupants. Both had blond hair and blue eyes like David, and both were slim and elegant, dressed in pastel skirt suits. Zita was the odd one out in her bright blue top and white skirt.

"David, how lovely to see you." The older woman stood and kissed both of David's cheeks.

"Mom, this is my girlfriend, Zita."

"It's a pleasure."

Zita smiled as she shook the woman's hand. "It's nice to meet you, Mrs. Randall."

"Call me Fay. Mrs. Randall is my mother-in-law." She

shuddered delicately.

Zita grinned as her tension evaporated. She liked the woman already.

"Zita, this is my sister, Lorelei."

"I love your top," Lorelei said. "That color looks fantastic on you."

"Thank you." Zita took a seat.

The waiter arrived to take their drinks order and when he left, Fay said, "How did you meet my David?"

"At a symposium."

"Zita's sister is Carolina Flanagan," David told them. "She was speaking at the event."

"Oh, I met Carolina at a fundraiser last year," Lorelei said.

Zita was curious about David's sister. She guessed Lorelei was about the same age as her, but David hadn't said much about her. "What is it you do, Lorelei?" Zita asked.

"Do? Well, I'm on a number of boards and I play tennis twice a week." Her smile seemed fake.

"Which boards?"

"There's one for breast cancer research, another that deals with scholarships for disadvantaged youth, and also one that addresses homeless issues."

"That's fantastic. It must be great to help in that way."

"Yes. It keeps me busy." She laughed as she said it, but there was something in her eyes that made Zita think she wasn't happy.

"You do wonderful work for the different charities you support," Fay said.

"It's hardly work."

Zita knew that expression. She'd seen it in the mirror. "I've been helping my mother with our charity Casa Flanagan for years, but sometimes it feels as if I'm not actually doing anything."

"Then you know how I feel." Lorelei smiled. "It seems like forever since I was at Harvard and actually challenged by anything."

Zita acknowledged the twinge of offense and didn't comment further.

"You never showed any interest in working before," David

said.

"You're going to be CEO. There's no point if I can't be the best."

Zita glanced at David. Did that mean Lorelei wanted to work at Dionysus? Maybe this was his chance to step down.

David's mouth dropped open. "You want to be in charge of Dionysus?"

"I'd love to be, but we both know that's not going to happen."

"I never realized," he said. "We should talk."

Lorelei frowned. "What about?"

"You working at Dionysus."

"You're not listening, David. I want to be CEO or nothing."

He hesitated and looked at Zita. She nodded to him. "I don't want to be CEO."

Both Fay and Lorelei stared at David as if he'd grown another head. Zita squeezed his hand and he smiled.

"Since when?" Lorelei asked.

"I've never really wanted it, but I didn't think I had a choice."

Lorelei grinned. "You really mean it?"

He nodded. "We'll have to run it by Dad."

"That would be amazing. When do I start?"

"Oh dear," Fay said. "Warn me before you break the news to your father. I need to make sure I'm there to play peacekeeper."

"He'll come around," Lorelei said. "As long as there's a Randall in charge." She sounded confident.

David's shoulders relaxed and Zita grinned. It was the perfect outcome.

Their drinks were served, and the conversation drifted to other topics.

When it was time to go, Zita said goodbye to Fay and Lorelei and they walked out of the restaurant.

"Holy hell," David said when they got into the car. "I can't believe that just happened."

"How do you feel?" Zita asked.

"Slightly terrified." He tapped his palm on the steering wheel.

Zita squeezed his thigh. "I'm sure you'll be great at whatever you decide to do."

"I don't know about that, but I'm excited about the challenge."

They drove in silence for a while before David cleared his throat. "Are you free next weekend?"

"I'm not sure . . ."

"Can you ask your mom? Check if she can spare you for the whole weekend?"

Zita frowned. "Why?"

"I thought we could go away. It's Valentine's Day after all."

She'd never paid much attention to Valentine's Day, but the idea of getting away for a couple of days was extremely enticing. "Where to?"

"It's a surprise."

She raised an eyebrow at his grin. "All right. Give me a second." She dialed her mother's number. "Mama is there anything important going on next weekend?"

"No, *niñita*. Why?"

"David's invited me away for the weekend."

"Go. Have fun."

Zita grinned, her heart light. "All right. Thanks, Mama." She hung up. "I can go."

"Great. I'll organize everything. Make sure you're packed and ready to go by midday on Friday."

Excitement swirled in her stomach. She was going to spend a whole weekend with David. "What will I need to pack?"

"Umm." He was quiet for a moment, thinking. "A nice, dressy outfit, and then something casual."

"How nice? Where are we going?" He had to be more specific.

"Something like you wore to Carly's engagement party will be fine."

That was a bit fancy. What did he have planned? She glanced at his face. "You're not going to tell me anything else are you?"

"No."

Zita smiled. The idea of a surprise weekend away was thrilling. Her heart lifted and her spirits rose.

She couldn't wait.

***

Zita was at the dining room table sorting through the documentation for Teresa when her cell phone dinged, indicating she had a message. She grabbed her phone and checked the social media message. The sender's name jumped out at her.

Sean Flanagan.

She gasped and touched the screen to open the message. No, she couldn't read it here in case someone walked in. Hurrying to her bedroom, she then shut the door and sat on her bed. She shut her eyes to control the nervous excitement. It might just be a polite message to say they weren't related and she'd made a mistake.

There was only one way to find out.

She opened her eyes and read the message. Her mouth dropped open. Her head spun and she clutched the bedspread. Breathing quickly, she read the message a second time to make sure she hadn't misunderstood.

The words were clear.

I think I'm your half-brother.

She shook her head, denying it, but his resemblance to her father was why she'd contacted him in the first place.

What should she do?

Reading through it again, she registered the details — his mother hadn't known she was pregnant when Brendan had left Ireland, and no one knew where he'd gone.

Zita's heart went out to him. She'd been upset about not remembering her father, but to not even know where he was, if he was alive or dead, would have been awful. And she'd mentioned he'd died in her message to him.

She needed to talk to him, to find out more before she mentioned him to her mother or sisters. How would Carmen feel about her husband having an illegitimate child in Ireland?

Zita typed out a reply. *We should talk. What's your number?*

She hit send.

She got to her feet as a response arrived with his contact details. Should she call him now? It all felt a little rushed, but she put herself in his shoes. If he knew nothing about his father, he'd be eager to learn more.

Checking the time, Zita realized she had another hour before Carmen would be home. She video-called him.

As his face appeared on the screen, her heart hurt. It was like the home movie come to life. "Hi," she said. "This is kind of surreal."

He blinked a few times. "It is. When I got your message I couldn't believe it was true. It took me a while to work up the courage to contact you."

"I'm glad you did. So how old are you, Sean?"

"I'm thirty."

Zita did the calculations. It was quite possible he was only a few months older than Carly. Their parents had met a few days after Brendan had arrived in El Salvador. They'd married a week later, and Carly was conceived not long after. Zita sighed. "This is so weird. What do you know about your father?"

Sean reached for something and held it up in front of the camera. "This is a photo of my father, taken right before he left Ireland."

It was definitely him. Her father.

"I didn't know much about him growing up. I had his name, and there had been rumors he'd been a terrorist."

Zita gasped. "What?" No. Not her father.

"It wasn't true," he assured her. "He was accused of helping the IRA in the eighties. There was some kind of conspiracy charge and he fled the country. It wasn't until a year later they found the real culprit, but by then no one knew where he'd gone."

She let out a deep breath. He was innocent. Had Carmen known why he'd left Ireland? "So Papa didn't know about you?"

Sean shook his head. "He was accused before my mother was even aware she was pregnant."

That made it easier to understand. She would have hated to find out her father had abandoned his son. "Did she ever search for him?" If she'd loved him she would have been heartbroken.

"No. They'd only just met and with the rumors flying around, she didn't want to." He ran a hand through his hair. "I tried to find out more about him when I was a teenager, but he hadn't even told his friends where he was going. I had no idea how to find him."

"Does Papa have any family left in Ireland?"

"A great uncle and great aunt, a couple of second cousins. No one close." He hesitated. "Can you tell me about him?"

Zita nodded. "Brendan married my mother within a week of meeting her. It was love at first sight, and they had three daughters. I'm the youngest." She swallowed hard. "I'm sorry to have to tell you this, but when I was three, Papa was murdered."

Sean's eyes widened.

"He was in the wrong place at the wrong time. El Salvador was getting more dangerous and we were in the process of immigrating to the United States, but the approval didn't come through in time to save Papa. We moved as soon as it did. We all live in Houston now."

Sean's shoulders slumped.

"I'm so sorry," Zita said, but the words felt useless. Her brother hadn't known his father and now he never would. "He's buried in El Salvador."

"I'll never actually meet him."

Tears welled in Zita's eyes. "I barely remember him, but we have photographs and home movies . . . I can show you."

"Could I see a photo now?" He hesitated. "You know, just to make sure we're talking about the same person?"

"Of course." Zita should have thought of that. She was a stranger contacting him out of the blue. She reached over and grabbed a family photo from her bedside table. "Can you see this?" She held it up.

"Yeah. So which one is you?"

"I'm the baby. The others are Bridget and Carly." She pointed them out. "They're going to freak out when I tell them about you."

He smiled. "I'm pretty amazed myself. I could have three sisters."

"And I could have a brother." Zita blinked away tears.

Sean hesitated. "Do you think we should confirm it? Like do DNA testing or something? I don't know how hard that is."

He was right. She had to be sensible, confirm they were related before they went any further. "That's a good idea. I'll make some calls this afternoon."

After exchanging email addresses they hung up.

Zita sat there for a moment, not quite able to believe it.

She had a brother.

***

By Friday, Zita had found a company who could test their DNA and interpret the results. She'd arranged for them both to be sent kits, but had only confided in David about Sean. She didn't want to tell her family until she had proof. She pushed thoughts of Sean out of her head as she waited for David to pick her up for their weekend away.

Despite cajoling and pleading, Zita hadn't been able to convince David to tell her where they were going. She didn't know if she was packing the right clothes, so she'd ended up over-packing. She had enough clothes to last two weeks.

"David's here," Carmen called.

Zita grabbed her suitcase and lugged it downstairs. At David's raised eyebrows, she said, "I wasn't sure what to bring."

He grinned and kissed her, and she stopped worrying.

"You take care of my baby," Carmen said to him.

"I will," David promised and handed her a piece of paper. "Details of where we'll be in case you need to contact us."

Zita reached for the paper in her mother's hand, but Carmen held it behind her back. "No. Don't ruin the surprise."

David took her hand. "Come on. We need to go." He lifted her suitcase, grunting a little at the weight.

"I'll see you Sunday, Mama."

Carmen was reading the note from David, eyes wide. She looked up and smiled. "Have fun, *niñita*."

Zita was desperate to find out where they were going, but David was already tugging her toward the car.

He put her case in the trunk and they got in. "Your dad's not upset about you taking half a day off work?"

"I've got time owing."

They drove around the city until they came to an airfield. When David turned in, Zita glanced at him. "We're not flying somewhere." They couldn't possibly. It would be far too expensive.

"Aren't we?" There was a smirk on his lips.

"David. You can't be serious. I can't afford to fly somewhere for the weekend." Dismay filled her. They hadn't discussed costs, but she'd already decided she would pay her share.

"I can."

"Don't be silly. I can't let you pay for me."

"Of course you can. It's my pleasure to take you away." He pulled into a hangar and parked. Inside was a plane, with Dionysus Oil and Gas written on the side.

"You're using the company plane?" She was sure there'd be some rules in place about this. She didn't want David getting into trouble. "Won't your dad flip out?"

"Executives get the use of the jet once a year, as long as it's not needed by the company."

Some of her concern subsided as she got out of the car and looked up at the sleek, white plane. A little shiver of excitement went through her. They could be going anywhere.

At the foot of the stairs to the jet, a flight attendant came to greet them. "Mr. Randall, nice to see you again."

"Hi Lewis. This is Zita Flanagan."

"Ms. Flanagan, a pleasure."

When they climbed the stairs, a woman appeared in the doorway. "We're ready to leave when you are, Mr. Randall."

"Great. Zita, this is Captain Johnson. She's our pilot for the flight."

"Nice to meet you."

Zita followed the pilot inside the plane. She'd told herself she wasn't going to stare, but she couldn't help it. There were a dozen plush leather seats, each with a table to work on, and the carpet under her feet was soft. It screamed luxury and comfort.

"Where would you like to sit?" David asked her.

She shook her head, still not quite believing it. "Anywhere."

He pointed to two seats in the middle. "How about here? Would you like the window seat?"

"Yes, please." She sunk into the leather and buckled the seatbelt. Lewis was securing the door and Captain Johnson had gone into the cockpit to prepare for takeoff. "David, this is unbelievable. I thought we were going to some cabin for the weekend."

He ran his hand down her arm. "I wanted to spoil you."

Zita's heart swelled. No one had ever wanted to spoil her before. Was it any wonder she'd fallen in love with him? "So are you going to tell me where we're going now?"

"Nope."

It didn't matter. Wherever it was, it was going to be somewhere she'd never been before.

The engines hummed and she gripped the armrests of her chair to stop herself from bouncing up and down in excitement. They were really doing this.

"Are you a nervous flier?" David asked.

"I don't know. I was three the last time I flew anywhere."

"No kidding?"

"I'm so excited." She grinned at him as the plane taxied out of the hangar. Then after a moment's pause, the engines roared to life and the plane hurtled along the runway. This was actually happening! Her ears popped as they lifted off the ground and climbed to cruising altitude. Zita peered out of the window at the ground getting smaller and smaller beneath them. "That was so much fun."

He shook his head. "I've never thought of takeoff as being fun."

"You don't like it?"

"No, I've just never paid it any attention."

"I guess you fly a lot."

"Yes. These days, it's mostly for business, but we used to go on family vacations when I was a kid."

Zita had dreamed of flying somewhere exotic when she was a child, but she'd always thought it was just that — a dream. Until now. The plane leveled out and she peered out of the window. "We're flying northwest."

He smiled but said nothing.

Lewis came down the aisle and asked, "Would you like a drink? Champagne? A cocktail, perhaps?"

Zita glanced at David.

"Anything you want," he said.

"A cocktail, please." She felt like being decadent. "Something fruity, if you have it."

Lewis nodded and turned to David.

"I'll have whatever she's having, and can we have some

cheese and fruit, please?"

"Certainly." He disappeared into what Zita assumed was the galley.

"This is amazing," she said.

"I'm glad you like it. There's in-flight entertainment, or a bunch of books in the compartment over there, or if you want, you can take a nap in the bedroom at the back."

"There's a bedroom?" Her smile grew wider.

"Yes."

She got to her feet and held out her hand. "You should show it to me immediately."

His eyes widened and then he grinned. "If you insist."

***

After she and David had made sure the bed was satisfactory, they returned to the sitting area. As they sat, Lewis appeared with their drinks and food. He must have been waiting for them. A flush spread over Zita's cheeks. "Thank you."

"You're welcome." Lewis winked at her and she laughed.

She took a sip of the watermelon concoction; it was extremely refreshing. She could get used to this service. "How long until we land?"

"Tired of flying already?" David asked.

"Just wondering whether there's time for another nap," she said, enjoying his wicked grin in response.

"Let's finish our food first," he suggested.

They chatted as they ate, and Zita relaxed from the slight buzz the cocktail gave her. She was flying far enough away that she wouldn't be available if her mother needed her. She acknowledged the anxiety and reminded herself both Carly and Bridget were in Houston and could help.

As the plane descended and the captain told them to put on their seatbelts, Zita checked the time. They'd been flying for over four hours. She glanced out of the window at the lights of a city. But which city she had no idea. The plane banked and Zita gasped.

The bright lights of the strip were clear even in the dusk. Las Vegas.

She threw her arms around David. "Thank you! I've always

wanted to go to Vegas."

"I know." He kissed her. "Wait until you see where we're staying."

"I don't care where we're staying. The fact we're in Vegas is enough."

"In that case, let me change the booking to a motel off the strip," he joked.

She swatted him. "You know what I mean."

When the plane came to a complete stop, Zita got to her feet and hugged David again. "Whatever happens, thank you for this weekend. Thank you for taking me away from the madhouse for a couple of days."

"You're most welcome."

Lewis opened the door and lowered the stairs. Zita stepped outside where a sleek black limousine was parked.

"Compliments of the hotel," David said, gesturing her forward.

This was so far removed from the life Zita was used to. She greeted the driver who held the door open for her, and she slid inside the car. It was so spacious. She scooted over for David, and in almost no time, they were on their way.

Zita held his hand as they drove into town. There was so much light, all bright and flashy, with people walking the streets. It was bustling and magical.

They pulled into a hotel and the foyer took Zita's breath away. It was so lavishly decorated in gold tones and everything sparkled. The centerpiece was a gorgeous Roman statue and huge artworks covered the walls. She walked up to the registration desk with David. The cost of the lobby alone would be enough to feed a family in El Salvador for several years.

She frowned. It was such a lavish lifestyle. Was it right to spend so much money on herself when there were so many people around the world who had nothing? In her heart she knew that just giving poor people money wasn't the solution, there had to be education and support systems and more, but it didn't stop her from feeling a little guilty.

David took her hand and they followed the bellhop to the elevator. The doors opened onto a plush hallway. They walked down the corridor and the man paused outside a door, holding it open as Zita walked inside.

Her jaw dropped. She wasn't quite sure where to look first. The bed was enormous, covered with crisp white sheets and mountains of golden pillows all dying to be jumped on. On one side, were three cushy couches surrounding a coffee table, holding a vase of the most beautiful array of white and yellow roses, and the flat screen television on the wall had to be at least fifty inches.

"What do you think?" David asked.

She turned to him and noticed the bellhop was gone. "This is amazing, David. I've never seen anything like it in real life."

"I may have splurged," he admitted. "I wanted you to have the best."

It most certainly was the best. She hugged him, holding him tightly as her emotions flew all over the place. She didn't care about the room or the private plane, she loved him for himself, but the fact he wanted to spoil her made her all gooey inside. She would push her guilt to the side and enjoy the weekend for what it was.

"If you think this is good, wait until you check out the bathroom," he murmured in her ear.

She lifted her head. "Is the bath big enough for two?"

He grinned. "Why don't you check?"

She kissed him quickly and then moved to the bathroom. She stared. "*Feck*," she breathed. The bathtub was enormous, large and oval with spa jets, and next to it the shower recess with its two shower heads had to be big enough for a basketball team. It said opulence and indulgence all at once. "I have no words."

He chuckled. "I haven't made any dinner reservations yet. I thought you might want to choose."

She wasn't hungry. She wanted to soak in the tub, preferably with David. "I choose a bath with a naked boyfriend." She wound her hands around his neck and kissed him. "Is that all right?"

"Whatever you want." He kissed her back hard and lust speared through her. Perhaps they could do something else before the bath.

She stripped off her T-shirt and reached for his belt, backing him up against the bathroom wall. "I want you."

Chapter 15

David sank into the warm bubbles and pulled Zita toward him so she lay against his chest. The sex had been hard and fast, and had left them both satisfied.

Zita sighed as the water reached her chin. "This is amazing." She ran her hands down his legs and he stirred.

Would he ever get enough of her? He wrapped his arms around her and placed his hands on her stomach, kissing the top of her head. She felt so right against him. Her body fit to his, and was warm and lithe. "I'm glad you're enjoying it."

"How could I not?" She lifted his legs so they curled around her. "I've got my sexy boyfriend all to myself for the whole weekend." She sounded contented.

He was relieved. He'd worried she might have been too concerned about what was happening at Casa Flanagan to relax. Watching her excitement over the plane and the hotel room had made him realize how lucky he'd been in his life. He took this kind of luxury for granted, and her reaction had humbled him.

He massaged her shoulders.

"David, that feels incredible." Zita tipped her head to give him better access.

He loved how responsive she was. She made him feel good about himself, and he'd been missing that. His relationships until now had been so superficial.

"I might stay in this bath forever."

He chuckled. "The water will get cold eventually."

"All right then, but I'm not leaving this room," she said, her voice low.

"We can stay here the whole weekend if you want," he told her. "The room service menu is good."

"We should definitely get room service for dinner."

"Whatever you want." He pressed a kiss against her neck.

"Careful, if you're too agreeable, it might go to my head." She sat up and turned around, lying with her back on the opposite side of the tub. She took his foot and started massaging it. "You deserve some pampering as well."

Her fingers felt so good, but he didn't need pampering — that wasn't the point of the weekend. He tried to take his foot away, but she held it tight.

"You said whatever I want," she said. "And I want to pamper you."

He couldn't argue. "All right." He picked up one of her feet and started massaging.

She grinned. "You can't help yourself, can you?"

"No. I love touching you." The emotion that came with the realization was so strong he closed his eyes. He'd never felt so strongly about someone before. Opening his eyes, he looked directly at Zita. It hit him like a punch in the gut.

He loved her. He wanted to spend the rest of his life with her.

Loving her was like having the happiness of every brilliant day of his life rolled into one.

He frowned. But what if she didn't feel the same way? They hadn't known each other for very long.

Zita closed her eyes, and leaned her head back. "It feels so good."

He ignored his concerns. She was right, it did feel good, right, content.

He would bask in their weekend together and tell her how he felt when the moment was right.

***

Was it was possible to overdose on indulgence? If so, Zita was in danger of doing so. After their bath the night before, they'd ordered room service and spent the night talking. Now she was snuggled among a mountain of pillows and a thick quilt, watching David sleep. He looked so peaceful, and her heart swelled. He'd done all of this for her. He had to care for her to go to so much effort.

Not able to resist, she brushed the hair off his face and pressed a kiss against his cheek. His eyes opened and he smiled at her. "Morning, beautiful."

Her heart sang. "Good morning, sleepyhead."

He stretched. "What time is it?"

"Only eight." But she wanted to make the most of their time together.

He pulled her close, his hand running down her side, and her whole body woke up. "What do you want to do today?"

Sex was definitely on the agenda, but she didn't want him to miss out on doing something he wanted to do. "Do you have a preference?"

He shook his head. "I've been to Vegas before."

Of course he had. "Is there anything you'd recommend?"

"Why don't we go to the concierge after breakfast and see what's on offer?"

"Good idea."

They got up and showered, taking advantage of the two shower heads and unlimited hot water before going down to the lavish buffet breakfast in one of the hotel's restaurants. Every breakfast food imaginable was available, and by the time Zita finished tasting a bit of this and that, she was stuffed.

Afterward, they spoke with the concierge and he gave them pamphlets for shows and tours. One of the circus shows caught Zita's eye and she read the information.

"We could ask if there are still tickets," David said.

"All right."

As the concierge called to reserve seats, another brochure caught her eye. She grinned. "We should definitely do this. I've always wanted to try it."

David raised an eyebrow. "A Segway tour?"

"Yeah. Don't you think it looks like fun?"

"I can vouch that it's fairly easy to do," the concierge said. "I've booked you two tickets for the nine-thirty showing of the circus. Would you like me to check if the Segway tour has any availability?"

David was frowning at the brochure. He didn't want to do it. Zita ignored her disappointment. "Don't worry. I can do it another time."

"No," David said with a sigh. "We'll do what you want, though I've got to warn you, I've never been great on two wheels."

Intrigued, she asked, "You don't like bikes either?"

"Too many falls as a kid." He turned to the concierge. "Can you get us a couple of tickets?"

After they were booked, Zita arranged a couple's massage for the afternoon, just in case it was harder than they expected. They had only a few minutes before being picked up, so they dashed back to their room to get their things.

On the way back down, Zita got an attack of the guilts. David had grown quiet. "We can cancel," she said, bringing her arms around him. "If you don't want to go, we can always do something else."

"Don't be silly." He hugged her back. "I'm just worried my manliness rating will plummet." He kissed her nose.

She laughed. "You'll always be manly to me."

"Let's just wait and see."

It didn't take long to reach the location and run through the instructions. Zita listened carefully and then leaned forward to get the machine moving. After a couple of false starts, it was surprisingly easy. She glanced back at David to find him doing donuts in the practice area. Relief flooded her. She laughed. "You're getting the hang of it."

"Who knew it would be so easy? I've got to get me one of these. Beats walking to work."

Pleased it wasn't as bad as he'd feared, Zita relaxed and tested out the machine. When the rest of their tour group arrived, they set off down Fremont Street learning about the history of Las Vegas via a headset in their helmets. The day was overcast and cool, so it was pleasant rolling along the street and seeing some of the iconic buildings Zita had seen in movies. David rolled next to her, pointing out things of interest and laughing. She was glad she'd chosen to do this. He looked like he was having fun.

When the tour was over, they had lunch at a little Indian restaurant. When the waiter had taken her order, Zita asked, "Are you really going to get a Segway?" The tour guide had said they were expensive, way out of her budget.

"I might. It was a lot of fun. Thanks for suggesting it."

"I'm glad you enjoyed it."

"It was a blast." He chuckled. "I always thought I'd be too uncoordinated."

She tilted her head to the side. "You never struck me as the uncoordinated type."

"That's because I've done nothing athletic in front of you."

"I wouldn't say that." She winked at him and he grinned.

"I might have coordination in some areas."

"I'll say." She sipped her cocktail.

He blushed a little.

Zita adored him. He was such a gorgeous mix of confidence and humility. She took hold of his hand. "Thank you for bringing me to Vegas."

"Thank you for coming."

Their meals arrived and they chatted. She wanted to tell David how she felt about him, but she didn't want to ruin the weekend if he freaked out. Normally, she didn't hesitate to tell people she loved them, but this was too precious, too scary, too real.

But she wouldn't be able to keep it a secret for much longer.

***

It took Zita a couple of days to get back into the rhythm of Casa Flanagan when they returned from Las Vegas. Elena was getting more emotional each day as her hearing drew closer. She oscillated between clinging to Xaviera and not letting anyone near her, to not wanting anything to do with the baby.

On Wednesday, both Carmen and Zita sat down with Elena while Xaviera was sleeping.

"*Niñita*, we know you are anxious about your application," Carmen began. "But you need to decide what you want to do about Xaviera."

"She's my baby. I will keep her."

"You will keep her even if you get deported?" Carmen asked.

Elena hesitated. "My parents wouldn't be happy." She bit her lip.

"Elena, there are many cases where a parent is deported, even though their child is an American citizen. The child cannot apply on behalf of their parent until they are adults," Zita told her.

Elena's eyes widened. "They would separate a family?"

Zita nodded. "Make your decision about what you want to do with Xaviera, not based on your application to stay, but on whether you want to raise her." She touched Elena's arm. "It's a very big commitment and you're still young."

"If you want to keep her, we will support you like we are supporting Alejandra," Carmen said. "But if you want to give her up for adoption, we will make sure she goes to a good home."

Elena's eyes filled and she burst out crying. "You think I am a bad person," she sobbed. "But I never wanted her. I was raped so many times, I don't even know who her father is."

Zita pulled Elena close. "You're not bad. You were assaulted and Xaviera was a result. That doesn't mean you have to love her."

"I do love her," Elena sobbed. "I just don't want to take care of her. I see Alejandra with Julio and she loves spending every minute with him. I want to be free."

Carmen squeezed Elena's hand. "You can choose, *niñita*. If you give Xaviera up, you need to understand you may never see her again. But if you keep her, you have to be consistent in her care and she must come first. Being a parent means making compromises and not always being able to do what you want to do."

Elena hiccupped as her tears slowed.

"You don't need to decide now," Zita said. "Take your time and think about what you want, and tell us when you're ready."

"I don't want to keep her," Elena whispered, her eyes wide as she waited for their reaction. She took a deep breath. "But I want the best for her. Can we find her a loving family?"

Zita's heart cracked at the pleading look on Elena's face. "If you are sure."

She nodded with no hesitation. "I'm sure."

"I'll make some phone calls," Carmen said.

Zita hugged the girl, her heart sore for the choice Elena had to make and the baby she was going to lose.

Later that day, Teresa hurried into the room where Zita was feeding Julio. Tears streamed down her face.

"What's wrong?" Zita asked, suppressing a sigh. Teresa had become increasingly anxious about her mother and sister, now their application had been approved.

"We need to call Mama," Teresa said. "I am sure something bad has happened."

"Like what?"

"I don't know. It's a feeling, a dread in my stomach."

Zita did sigh this time. This was the fifth 'feeling' Teresa had had this week. "Teresa, we can't call your mother. Someone will get suspicious if we're constantly calling her. You need to trust Fernando is keeping an eye on them. In less than a week, they'll both be here."

"You don't know what it's like. They could be doing awful things to my sister!"

That was true, and there wasn't a damn thing they could do from here, except pray Manuela's age would protect her. Zita patted the couch next to her. "Sit down." Julio had finished his bottle so she placed it on the coffee table and shifted him so she had one hand free. She took hold of Teresa's hand. "It's difficult to wait. I know how easy it is to imagine all the nasty things that could happen, but we can't infiltrate the place where Manuela is being kept, not without great danger to both Manuela and whoever tries to rescue her. The best plan is the one we have — to rescue Manuela when she's sent home for her birthday."

"I'm so scared."

"I know, *niñita.* It's not long now, and they'll be safe." Zita pulled the girl toward her and hugged her. "You can hold on for a few more days."

Teresa sniffed and nodded.

"Can you take Julio for me?" Zita asked, hoping that if she gave her something to do, Teresa would stop obsessing.

Teresa held out her hands and Zita passed the baby over.

"I'll call Fernando tonight for an update," Zita said.

"Thank you." Teresa walked out of the room, cooing to Julio.

Zita let out her breath. This day had been an emotional rollercoaster. All the tension that had drained from her during her weekend in Vegas was now back with a vengeance.

Her cell phone rang and relief filled her when she saw David's name on the screen. "Hi."

"Are you free for dinner Saturday night?"

She smiled. "Sure."

"Full disclosure — it's kind of a family thing." He paused. "Dad's announcing his candidacy at a political dinner, and all of the family is expected to be there to support him. I thought you could be my plus one."

Zita screwed up her nose, glad he couldn't see her. The last thing she wanted to do was go to an event where it would appear that she supported Bob Randall, but it was nice David was inviting her.

"You'll sit at the family table for dinner," David went on, "and then there'll be speeches. I'm sure we can make an excuse for you to leave."

Now Zita felt bad. David was supporting his father, and she should be there for him, even if she didn't agree with his father's politics. "No, it's fine. I'll come. Thank you for inviting me."

"That's great!" He sounded so pleased.

"I'll drive. What time do you want me to pick you up?" If she had her car, she could escape if things got to be too much.

"Six. Do you want to stay overnight?"

"Sure. I'll see you then." She hung up and closed her eyes.

She was going to have to have some serious self-control on the night. Perhaps she'd invest in some duct tape for her mouth.

***

Zita stood in front of her wardrobe, her stomach in knots. She had nothing to wear, nothing that was appropriate for a conservative political dinner. She imagined the looks of disdain

167

she'd get if she wore one of her normal, brightly colored, slightly quirky outfits. Not a great way to make a good first impression.

If only she was the same size as Carly, then she could have borrowed something from her. Zita had no idea how formal it was. She shoved a couple of dresses along the rack. Were any of them appropriate?

This was ridiculous. If she didn't leave in the next half an hour she was going to be late. With a huff of disgust, she grabbed her phone and called David.

"I don't know what to wear," she said when he answered. "What's the dress code?"

"It's semi-formal."

She groaned. She rarely had a reason to go semi-formal. "What are you wearing?"

"A black suit."

She flicked through her clothes again. "What about the yellow dress I wore to Carly's engagement party?"

"The one that makes you look like an exotic flamenco dancer?"

She smiled at his description. "So that's a no. I'll check if Bridget or Daniella have anything I can borrow." She hung up and called Daniella. A few minutes later, she brought over a little black dress that fit.

Zita kissed her cheek. "Thank you. You're a life saver."

"My pleasure."

Zita quickly did her makeup and then slipped on a pair of low slung black heels. She trotted down the stairs. "Mama, I'm off."

Carmen glanced up. "You look lovely, if a little more sedate than usual."

"Best I keep things simple," Zita said. "It's a conservative dinner, and I want to make a good impression."

"There's no point hiding who you are, Zita. They'll find out eventually."

"I'm choosing to break it to them slowly." She doubted Bob would notice the effort, but she didn't want to create a scene. She kissed her mother's cheek and walked out the door.

The nerves returned as Zita parked at David's apartment. Family was important, and David had a good relationship with his father. If Bob didn't like her, would it hurt her relationship with David?

She took her overnight bag upstairs.

"You look gorgeous," David said.

"Thank you." She kissed him. "We should get going, the traffic is pretty bad."

"All right." After he locked his apartment, he took her hand and some of her nerves settled.

Once they were on the way, she asked, "Are there any subjects I shouldn't mention?"

David glanced at her. "That's probably a long list."

Her stomach rolled. She was no good at keeping her opinions to herself, especially if it was something she cared deeply about.

"Don't worry, Zita. I imagine most of the conversation will be surrounding Dad's candidacy. Neither of us will probably have to say anything."

"What about your mother and Lorelei?"

"They've always tended to let the men talk." He shrugged. "I imagine it's easier than trying to get a word in."

Zita couldn't imagine any of the women in her family being silent. Even the foster girls had their opinions. If she was supposed to be seen, but not heard, she might be in bigger trouble than she'd thought. She sighed. At least she'd have Fay and Lorelei to talk to.

The dinner was being held at a hotel not too far from David's apartment. When they arrived, only a few people were there. Zita recognized Bob, Fay and Lorelei, and assumed the dark-haired man standing with them was David's brother Grant. With them were Governor Harding and a woman she guessed was his wife.

The woman frowned when she saw Zita with David. Zita braced herself. She would be polite and non-confrontational.

"David. Zita." Fay smiled as she turned to them. She air kissed David's cheeks. "Lovely to see you." She held out her hand to Zita.

"How are you, Fay?" Zita asked as she shook it.

"Very well. Let me introduce you. This is my very close friend, Hillary Harding. Hillary, this is Zita."

Hillary gave Zita a cold nod.

Zita smiled at her, not sure why she was getting the cold shoulder.

"And if I can interrupt my husband . . ." Fay put a hand on Bob's arm. "Darling, meet David's date, Zita."

He turned. "Where do I know you from?" he asked.

Zita's stomach clenched. "We met briefly at the refugee symposium last year."

He continued to frown as if he was trying to remember.

"Zita, this is Governor Jesse Harding, and my youngest son, Grant."

She shook the older man's hand.

Bob clicked his fingers together. "You spilled wine on David."

"Yes." If that's all he remembered, it would be a good thing.

"You think we should let everyone in, don't you?"

Zita winced. She didn't want to get into a discussion about this. Not when she was on her best behavior. "Not at all, but I do support helping those whose lives are in danger."

David opened his mouth to say something, but Bob was faster. "Everyone says they're fleeing from something. They want to bring their problems over here, infect another country."

Be polite. "Some of my foster sisters want to be educated so they can go home and fight the issues there. They need a safe place where they can get an education."

He snorted. "I'll believe that when I see it."

Zita didn't comment. It was better if the subject was dropped.

"Bob, your guests are arriving," Fay said, nodding toward the entrance. "Perhaps we can discuss this later."

Bob glanced over and grunted. Then he straightened his posture, put on a huge grin, and went to meet his guests.

Zita let out a quiet breath. Was this an indication of what it would be like each time she saw Bob? Would all family events be full of this tension? Had it been a mistake to fall in love with David? He hadn't even stood up for her. He couldn't possibly still agree with his father, could he?

"Sorry," David murmured. "I didn't think he'd be so . . . rude."

She forced a smile. "It's fine."

"Zita, I must thank you for convincing David to step down," Lorelei said. "I've already started work at Dionysus." She was immaculately dressed in a navy blue evening dress.

Relieved at the change of subject, Zita said, "I didn't do anything." She took a glass of white wine from the waiter.

"Of course you did. He never mentioned it before he met you."

"She opened my eyes," David said, drawing her closer.

The warmth that spread through her was comforting.

"I wouldn't mention that to Dad," Grant said. "He's still annoyed about the time he's wasted on David." He laughed. "I'm going to find a real drink." He walked off.

Zita frowned. David hadn't mentioned anything about that.

"Ignore Grant," Lorelei said. "He's teasing."

Zita wasn't as sure, but she nodded.

At dinner, she kept her opinions to herself and her mouth shut. Luckily, most of the political conversation was between the men on the other side of the round table and she was able to shut it out by listening to Lorelei and Fay chatting. Then it was time for the speeches. Governor Harding stood and walked to the front. There were cameras from several television stations there, and the cameramen got to their feet to film.

The governor made his speech and then said, "I'm pleased to announce I am throwing my full support behind Bob Randall." He gestured for Bob to come to the front of the stage. Fay went with him, and Jesse explained who Bob was and what his qualifications were. Then he invited Bob to speak.

"It's a real pleasure to be asked to run for governor," Bob began. "The great state of Texas has a number of issues that need to be addressed." He went through some of his policies if he were to be elected. They'd only benefit the rich, but then it was only the wealthy at this dinner. Zita didn't say a word. She glanced at David, who was frowning.

"But the main issue I want to tackle is immigration."

Zita braced herself.

"We've got all of these people flooding into the country like a plague and it must be stopped." A couple of people cheered. "They're leeches on society, lawbreakers from the start, entering the country illegally and expecting us to pay millions of our taxpayers' dollars to support them and their hordes of children. They don't give anything back to society."

Zita's breath left her at his vitriol.

"Here, here," someone called.

"Some of the lies they tell are quite shocking." He held up a file. "My son has been gathering information about these illegal immigrants for me."

Zita stiffened. No. He wouldn't have.

David grabbed her hand. "I didn't give him that."

Zita barely heard him as Bob opened the file. "One young girl, a Beatriz Morales, told the government her stepfather beat her and she was allowed to stay, as if the Guatemalan government couldn't help a simple case of child abuse."

She was numb. David had been spying for his father? He'd said he was trying to change his father's mind. David squeezed her hand, but she shook him off, not quite comprehending.

"Another girl, Teresa Garcia, said she was forced into prostitution and had her application granted. But what's worse, her mother and sister, Johanna and Manuela Garcia, have also been approved, citing gang violence. How convenient."

More shouts of disgust.

The blood drained from Zita's face. Bob had mentioned the Garcias by name. If the information got back to El Salvador, Manuela and Johanna would be in danger. "Are those cameras live?"

"Zita, I didn't know he was going to say that," David said, his eyes pleading.

She pushed back her chair. "I said, are those cameras live?"

"I don't know."

She headed to the nearest cameraman. "When is this going out?"

He held up a finger for her to be silent.

She grabbed his arm. "Is this live?"

"No," he hissed. "But they are." He pointed to another station.

She swore and turned, crashing into David.

"Get out of my way." She pushed past him. She couldn't deal with him now, couldn't handle his betrayal. She had to call Carmen. They had to bring the rescue forward, just in case.

"Zita, wait. I didn't —"

She whirled. "I don't care. Right now I have to make sure your bigoted father didn't kill Teresa's family."

David reared back as if she'd struck him. "What?"

"This is going out live. He mentioned them by name and they're not safe yet. The gangs have supporters in the US. If someone sees this and tips them off. . ."

David paled. She refused to feel sorry for him. She'd trusted him, brought him into her life, exposed the girls to him, and he'd used the information to further his father's career. She wanted to be sick.

She rushed to the door as Bob called out, "There's my son, David." Swallowing the lump in her throat, she dialed her mother's number.

"Mama, you need to call Fernando. He needs to get Manuela and Johanna out tonight." She quickly explained what happened.

Carmen swore. "I'll call him now."

Zita handed her valet parking ticket to the attendant. David hadn't followed her.

She closed her eyes to stop the tears. He'd been using her to help his father. She'd been foolish to get involved with him, foolish to trust him, foolish to fall in love.

None of it had been real. Anger fired in her belly, burning up her tears. She was tempted to turn around and give David a piece of her mind, but she had to make sure the Garcias were safe.

Her car arrived and she got in and headed home.

<h1 style="text-align:center">Chapter 16</h1>

David stared after Zita, her words hitting him like a bullet. He'd endangered Manuela and Johanna.

"There's my son, David." Bob's words sunk into his consciousness and he turned at the applause. No, he hadn't endangered the family, his father had. He hadn't even realized Bob had picked up the file. He must have found it on David's desk at work.

"Without his diligence, I wouldn't have seen what was happening to our border security."

Anger flooded David. How could his father do this? How could he be so blind to the truth? How could he use him in this way?

David strode to the front of the room, his eyes not leaving his father. Bob's eyes narrowed as he got closer and his jovial smile faded.

"I've spoken enough for tonight," Bob said. "I hope I can count on your support." He waved, moving off the stage, and blocked David at the steps. "Whatever you have to say, save it for when we're alone," he said quietly. "I told them what they wanted to hear."

David's eyes widened. His father had known exactly what he was doing. This was all political. "You bastard," he said. "What you said is bullshit, but you don't care who you hurt. Let me tell you about those girls you so callously maligned. Beatriz is the sweetest girl you'd ever meet. She's still so trusting despite what she's been through." His chest was tight. "And Teresa's story is one you wouldn't wish on your worst enemy. Held against her will, prostituted out and controlled by a gang. Her opportunity to escape came after her arm had been *broken* while trying to protect herself."

"Keep your voice down," Bob growled.

David glanced around. The room was silent and everyone was watching them.

"The hell I will. Your ignorance of the situation might kill two women." People began to murmur. "Teresa's sister is being held by the gang. If they know she's leaving, they'll kill her. This isn't about politics, this is about someone's life." His voice broke. God, he hoped Manuela and Johanna were safe.

Bob glared at him.

"You really don't care, do you?" David shook his head.

"What I care about is that Mexican has turned your head the wrong way round. You would embarrass me like this rather than let people see the truth?"

David clenched his hands. "My head is just fine. That *American citizen* is the woman I love, the woman I want to marry."

Bob's eyes widened.

"What you did right now is unforgivable." He strode out of the room, pulling his cell phone out of his pocket. He dialed Zita's number, but she didn't answer.

Panic clutched his heart. He'd messed this up. He had to find her. Had to explain.

At the entrance, he stopped and swore. He didn't have his car.

Hailing a cab, he headed for his apartment.

***

Walking through the front door of Casa Flanagan, Zita was greeted with her mother trying to calm a hysterical Teresa.

Damn it. She should have thought about Teresa's reaction.

Carmen looked up. "Thank God you're back. Fernando's been shot."

Zita's breath left her. "What?"

"I called his number and his wife Maria answered. She said he was shot this afternoon, got caught in the crossfire of a gang attack and is in hospital. He's in critical condition. He can't help."

Teresa wailed.

There was no one else they could call at such short notice. Fernando was their only contact. There was only one other option. "I'll go."

"No." Carmen grabbed her arm. "You can't. It's too dangerous."

"I caused this mess. I'll fix it." Zita's heart raced as she strode into the kitchen and picked up the tablet from the bench. "I need a flight to San Salvador tonight."

"No, I won't let you go," Carmen said following her in.

"Mama, you don't have a choice." She flicked through the options. "There's one in just over two hours." She'd be cutting it close, but she should be able to make it. She handed the tablet to her mother. "Book me on it."

Carmen shook her head.

"Mama, *please*. I'm their only hope."

There were tears in Carmen's eyes.

"You know I'm right," Zita said.

Emotions ran across Carmen's face — fear, defiance and finally resignation. "All right."

"Thank you." Zita ran upstairs to grab her passport and change. She threw spare clothes in a backpack.

"It's booked," Carmen said as Zita returned downstairs.

"Thank you, Mama." She hugged her. "I need you to call Maria and tell her I'm coming. I'll need all the documentation from her."

"Please, baby, promise me you won't do anything tonight," her mother begged. "It's dangerous enough during the day, but that kind of neighborhood is deadly at night."

"I promise." She headed out the door.

***

David stopped at his apartment only long enough to grab his car, before heading for Casa Flanagan. He kept calling Zita, but she wouldn't pick up. He didn't blame her. He'd ignored his concerns about Bob.

On the freeway, he hit a traffic jam. He swore. He needed to get to Zita. Switching on the radio, he discovered it was a major crash and they were recommending people avoid the area. "Damn it."

By the time he arrived, two hours had passed since Zita had left the hotel. He raced up the front steps and pounded on the front door.

Carmen opened it. "David." She glared at him, blocking the entrance.

"Carmen, I'm so sorry. I didn't know Dad would do that, I promise you. Can I see Zita? I have to explain."

"No you can't." She burst into tears.

His heart jumped. Concerned, he put his arm around her and moved them into the house. "What's wrong?"

"She's gone to El Salvador," she sobbed.

"What?" Shock speared him forward, directing Carmen into the living room and onto the sofa. "Why?"

He listened to Carmen explain, the concern morphing into full-on dread. "You're telling me she's gone to get Manuela and Johanna out of the country, because the gang *shot* the person who was going to?"

She nodded. "There is no time to find anyone else. Not when someone might watch your father's broadcast and tip off the gang."

This was all his fault. He'd put the woman he loved in danger because his father was a jackass and he hadn't recognized it. "What time is her flight?"

"Soon. She'll be boarding."

He swore. "I'll go after her."

Carmen shook her head, tears pouring down her face. "You'll be too late. There isn't another flight until morning."

"I'll take the company jet, then." He prayed it was available. Carmen's eyes widened as David got to his feet. "Where's she staying?"

"I don't know. She said she'd call when she arrived."

His chest was so tight it was hard to breathe. "Then call me when she does, and tell her not to do anything until I get there." He wrote down his cell number for her.

Carmen clutched his hand. "Be careful. It's dangerous over there."

He nodded and left. As he ran down the steps, he called the pilot.

"We can be ready to go in three hours," Captain Johnson said.

Was it going to be fast enough? He hoped so. "I'll be there."

He wasn't letting Zita pay for his mistake.

***

Zita arrived in San Salvador not long after midnight and quickly made it through customs. After calling Maria and getting her address, she caught a cab to their house. On her way, she called Carmen to let her know she'd arrived safely.

"*Gracias a Dios*," her mother said. "You mustn't go anywhere until David arrives."

Her heart clenched. "David?"

"He's flying there to help you."

"No, Mama. He's caused enough trouble." She blocked the pain. "I don't need him here. He doesn't speak the language." She couldn't think of him. She had to keep her mind focused on Manuela and Johanna.

"Please, *niñita*. You can help each other."

Zita wasn't promising anything. "I've got to go. I've arrived." She hung up and paid the cab driver.

Maria opened the door and shepherded her inside. "Quickly, it is not safe to spend too much time outside at night."

Zita glanced behind her as she entered the house. The neighborhood was quiet. "Thank you for staying up. How is Fernando?"

"He woke before I left the hospital. He is going to be all right."

Zita breathed out a sigh of relief. "What happened?"

"Gang fight. Fernando was in the wrong place." She handed Zita an envelope. "This is everything."

Zita opened it and checked the information: passports, visas, tickets in Johanna and Manuela's names, plus a map of the area. "Thank you."

"Let me show you where you need to go." Maria took the

map and spread it out on her dining table. She pointed out the laundry where Johanna worked. "There's a hostel and a market nearby. The gang knows tourists bring in needed money, so they keep violence to a minimum."

Zita's skin was tight. She'd heard about how dangerous the areas were, and now she was going to see for herself.

"Fernando talks about his grandmother, Francesca, when he visits Johanna. He set it up so if he couldn't make it, someone else could go and use that as a code word."

"All right." She could remember that.

Maria hesitated. "Zita, you can pass for a tourist, but if you don't want to draw attention to yourself, you should dye your hair."

Of course. She didn't look like a Salvadoran.

"I have a color you can use." She smiled. "I use it to hide the gray."

Maria didn't look old enough to have to worry about gray hair, but Zita took the box she was offered.

"We could do it now, and you can stay the night here," Maria said. "You can start early in the morning when it is safer."

"Thank you. I'd appreciate it." She wasn't thrilled about the way Maria kept mentioning safety. Could she pull this off? Could she even get close enough to Manuela to speak to her, let alone rescue her?

She hoped so.

An hour later, with newly brown hair, Zita went to sleep in Maria's guest bedroom.

Zita's alarm woke her when it was still dark. She reached for her phone while her brain struggled to remember where she was. She was so damn tired. Why had she set her alarm for the middle of the night? Then it hit her.

She was in El Salvador.

It was early morning, and would soon be light. She needed to be ready to go when it was.

She dressed quickly. She needed a double-strength coffee to clear her head, and then she had to be at the laundry when Johanna started work so she could find out where they were keeping Manuela and somehow get them both away.

The house was quiet as she tiptoed into the kitchen to get a glass of water.

Someone banged on the front door and the noise made her jump. Who the hell was outside at this time of the morning? Maria hurried out in her dressing gown, her face pale.

"Zita, are you in there?"

She swore. It sounded like David.

"You know him?" Maria asked.

Zita went to the front door, peeking through the peephole to check. It was definitely him. She opened the door. "What are you doing here?" Her heart hurt. He looked as if he hadn't slept.

He frowned. "Zita? You've dyed your hair."

"What do you want?"

"Carmen told me where you were. I want to help."

Maria pulled him inside and shut the door behind him. Zita walked back to the kitchen without answering him.

"Please, let me explain," David said.

Zita closed her eyes for a moment before turning to him. She couldn't let herself be distracted. "I don't have time for explanations."

He ignored her. "I'm so sorry this happened, Zita. I had no idea Bob had taken my file."

Was he telling the truth? "Why did you even have a file?" She couldn't sit down. She paced the kitchen as Maria started making breakfast.

"It's what I always do when I work on something."

"And you showed it to your father?"

"He asked me about the cases and I had to check some information. He saw it then."

"You told him confidential information?" She shook her head, her heart more bruised than it had ever been.

"I trusted him. I wanted to show him he was wrong."

"And what did you think he was going to do with the information?"

"I thought he'd change his mind." David ran a hand through his hair and sighed. "I made a huge mistake, I know it. After you left, I confronted him in front of the whole room."

Zita raised her eyebrows. "How did that go down?"

He shrugged. "I didn't wait to find out. Mom called me

when she'd calmed Dad down. She's not going to tell Dad I've taken the company plane."

"What?" Her anger was fading and she clung on to it.

"It was the quickest way I could get here. Carmen was beside herself when I arrived at Casa Flanagan. I had to come after you. It was my fault this happened, and I couldn't bear it if anything happened to you."

He reached for her and she stepped back, knowing she couldn't let him touch her. She didn't want to feel anything at the moment. She needed to be numb.

"Stop. I need to focus on what I have to do."

"What *we're* going to do," he corrected her.

No. It was too dangerous to involve him. She didn't want him hurt. "You'll stick out as a foreigner."

"If he stays with the car, it could work," Maria said. "They do have some tourists in the area because of the hostel."

Zita swore. She didn't want him there.

"I can do that," he said quickly. "I hired a car from the airport."

"It would help you to have a fast getaway," Maria said. "Just in case."

The thought of David anywhere near the danger was terrifying. She still loved him.

"Please, Zita. Let me make amends for what I did."

She heard the plea in his voice. She hated this, but she had to be sensible. "You'll do exactly what I tell you without question?"

He nodded as Maria dished up breakfast.

She exhaled slowly. "All right. Let me show you the map."

As they ate, she pointed out the market and the laundry where Johanna worked.

"Locals get their fresh food there, and there are stalls selling tourist things for the nearby hostel," Maria said, pointing out the hostel.

"We can park there and I'll go through the market to the laundry," said Zita.

"I'm not letting you out of my sight," David said.

"You don't have a choice. You're too conspicuous. I'll give you some money and you can browse near where we park the car to make sure it doesn't get stolen."

They traced the route they would take, and the route to the airport. By the time they were done, they had finished breakfast and the sun was up.

"It's time to go," Zita said. She turned to Maria. "Thank you for your help. Give Fernando my love and tell him I hope he heals quickly."

Maria nodded. "Be safe, *niñita*."

Zita grabbed her backpack and followed David outside. He'd hired a mid-range white sedan, so hopefully it wouldn't stand out in the neighborhood they were heading to. She got in the passenger side with the map clutched in her hand.

They were silent for the first two blocks, except for Zita giving directions.

"Zita, after all of this is over, I hope you can forgive me." His voice was quiet. "I never meant to hurt anyone."

Tears sprang to her eyes. "Please, David. Not now." She swallowed past the lump in her throat. "I can't do this now." Her voice broke at the last word and he glanced over at her. She turned her head, blinking back the tears. "I need to focus."

"All right."

They continued in silence until David pulled into the street where the markets were located. Zita checked the map to orientate herself and took a deep breath. "Keep your phone with you. I'm going to find out where they're keeping Manuela, and we'll go from there."

David looked unhappy, but agreed.

The markets were noisy and bustling with people. The stalls were full of fresh produce as well as souvenirs for tourists. She left David by a stall selling jocote, and wandered through the aisles toward the laundry.

She carried her backpack so she could leave her spare clothes to be washed if she needed an excuse. The amber stucco on the building made it stand out, and there was a sign in the single window proclaiming it to be a laundry. Outside, a young man was smoking. Zita ignored him as she walked into the shop. Johanna was behind the counter. Zita recognized her from the passport photo. Out the back, a man was sitting on a crate, flicking through his phone.

"Can I help you?" Johanna asked.

"My grandmother Francesca says you do the best laundry in town," Zita said, hoping the code word would work.

Johanna's eyes widened and she glanced at the man behind her. She lowered her voice. "You are from Fernando?"

Zita nodded.

"What is wrong? Manuela's birthday isn't until tomorrow."

"I'm Zita. There's been a change of plan. We need to get you both out today. Where is she?"

Someone walked into the shop, and Johanna gaped, her eyes wide in fear. The guy was in his late twenties, with tattoos all over his arms. Zita ducked her head, hiding her face.

"Rodrigo," Johanna said.

"Manuela hasn't been behaving herself. She was very mean to one of my girls, so today she's going to stand with the lovelies."

"No," Johanna wailed, a sound so heart wrenching. "She's still a baby."

Zita had no idea who the lovelies were, but it clearly wasn't a good thing.

Rodrigo shrugged. "She should learn how to behave. She'll miss her birthday party as well. So sorry." He smirked and walked out as Johanna collapsed on the floor sobbing.

Zita's heart pounded, but she waited until he was gone before hurrying around the bench to comfort the woman.

"Shut her up." The guy who'd been sitting on the crate stood up and walked toward them. "You've got three minutes." He pulled a cigarette out of his pocket and went outside.

"Johanna, calm down. You have to tell me what's going on." Zita shook her. "I can help.

Johanna shook her head. "The lovelies are their prostitutes," she sobbed. "He means to sell her today."

Zita's breath left her. *Feck.* Manuela wasn't even thirteen. "Where do they do that?"

Johanna sniffed. "The red building. Two streets over."

"What time?"

She shrugged. "All the time."

That didn't help. "Is there someone else who knows more?"

She shook her head. "No one who will talk."

"All right. Stop crying. I'll think of something." If there was only someone she could trust. Someone who could hire Manuela.

She froze. David.

But that would put him in danger. If any of the gang's supporters had seen the footage . . . No, if they had, they'd be punishing Johanna right now.

This was their best chance. "I've got an idea. I think we can get her out, but you need to be ready to leave at any time." Zita helped her to her feet.

"It's no use," Johanna sobbed.

The man came back inside. "Is she still sniveling?" He raised his hand and Zita automatically stepped in front of Johanna.

"She's stopping."

The man scowled and backhanded Zita. She stumbled back into Johanna, blinking rapidly to clear her eyes and fight past the pain. *Feck.* He'd actually hit her.

"Know your place," he said and walked out the back.

Zita's cheeked burned, but she turned to Johanna. "Stop crying," she murmured.

The expression on the woman's face was pure desolation.

"I'll fix this." Zita hoped she could keep her promise.

Johanna didn't respond, but Zita couldn't wait until she recovered. She walked out and hurried across to the markets, her mind racing as she formulated a plan. She found David not far from where she'd left him.

"What the hell happened to you?" David exclaimed, reaching for her face.

"Shhhh," she said, brushing his hand away. "Listen to me. Manuela's done something to annoy the gang and they're pimping her out today."

He swore.

Zita took a breath, hating the words she had to say next. "I need you to hire her."

Chapter 17

"What?" David's mind couldn't keep up. Zita had returned with a nasty red mark on her cheek and he wanted to know who the hell had put it there.

"I need you to go into the brothel and hire Manuela. It's the only way we'll get her out." She pulled him toward the car. "I'll be with you as your translator. We can pretend you're into young girls and want the youngest they have."

The mere idea made him feel ill. "There's got to be another way."

"There isn't." She glared at him. "You said you wanted to help."

This was his fault. They wouldn't be in this mess if he hadn't recorded all of the information. "What's the plan?"

Zita kept walking, pointing to the hostel across the road. "First, we need to get a room."

A few minutes later, they were in a private room in the hostel. Zita dragged a change of clothes out of her backpack.

"We'll go into the brothel together," she said, stripping off her T-shirt. "I'll tell them you heard you can get young girls there. You're looking for the younger the better, and for a virgin you'll pay top price." She shrugged a new top on. "This is Manuela."

Zita took a passport out of her backpack and showed him

the photo. The girl looked similar to Teresa, and was so damned young. David felt ill. How could anyone do that to her?

"You'll choose her and then what happens next will depend on what they do." She changed her skirt for jeans. "I don't know if they let the girls leave the brothel. If they want you to stay there, you need to make a fuss, say you've got a clean room here and you want privacy or something like that." She waited for his response.

This was real. He had to hire a twelve-year-old girl from a brothel. His stomach swirled as he nodded.

"Then we'll take her straight to the car, grab Johanna on the way past and get out of here."

"What if they send someone with us?" He doubted the gang would let Manuela go alone.

"Then you'll have to come here." She paused, glancing around the room and then went to the window and peered out. "You can climb out."

David walked over and stuck his head out. The room they were in was part of a row of three, and they were at the far end. There was a small strip of grass between it and the next row of rooms. He and Manuela could climb out, walk along the back and then dash between the two rows, hoping the person guarding wouldn't see them. "It's a long shot. Manuela won't trust me, and I don't speak enough Spanish to tell her what's going on."

Zita bit her lip. "I'll write a note, and I have a photo of Teresa on my phone. I'll send it to you." She pressed a few buttons on her phone.

David opened the door as he thought it through. The distance between the rows of rooms was at least twelve feet. "If the guard is looking our way, we're screwed."

Zita came out. "I'll distract him. I'm sure I can talk to him for a few minutes, wait until you go past and then make my excuses."

"Hell no." He shook his head. "I'm not leaving you alone with any gang member." There was no telling what they'd do to her.

"Have you got a better idea? I can't come into the room with you." She moved back inside and he followed her.

She was right. He couldn't think of another way around it. "Then what?"

"I'll meet you at the car and we'll get Johanna."

"And if someone else spots us?"

She took his hand. "Your priority is Manuela. Get her away from here. If we're spotted, or have to split up, head for the airport."

There was no way he would leave Zita behind. David shook his head, opening his mouth to refuse, but she covered it with her hand, pleading with her eyes.

"I speak Spanish, and Johanna knows this neighborhood. Chances are if you get spotted, people will chase you and not remember Johanna until after I've got her." Zita took her hand away. "The laundry is on the other side of the market. We can blend in there, then get a ride out to the airport. We both have our phones, so we can meet up there."

David's chest was so tight he could barely breathe. "I don't like this."

"Neither do I, but it's the best I can come up with. Are you ready?"

He was never going to be ready. He wanted to tell Zita how much he loved her, but it would sound like he didn't think they'd get out of there alive. He nodded once. "Let's go."

***

Zita left her backpack in the car, hoping no one would steal it while they were away. Then she walked toward the brothel with David. Her heart raced and every step felt like she was walking toward her own execution.

As the red building came into view, she said, "Let me do the talking. I'll translate any questions they have. You just need to pay." She'd given him the cash while they were at the car.

There were two men guarding the door.

"He's after a girl," Zita said in Spanish, jerking her head at David.

They looked David up and down, grinned and let them in. Inside the dim, narrow hallway Zita took a breath to brace herself. The scent of dirt and sweat filled her nostrils and she screwed up her nose.

Slowly, she walked down the hallway, glad she wasn't alone. She entered a large room with a wooden desk in the center. A tall, broad-shouldered man with a mustache and gang tattoos sat behind it. As Zita strode over to him, she took in the room. The paint on the walls was yellowed and peeling, and there were half a dozen plastic chairs around the edge. A teenage boy lounged in one, and there was a flight of stairs up to the next floor.

Mustache man glanced up from cleaning his gun. "What do you want?"

She dragged her eyes away from the weapon. "We're here for a girl."

The man grinned widely. "What kind of girl?"

She translated for David.

"The younger the better." He winked at the man, and Zita had to take a second to control her surprise at his authentic leer before she translated.

The man called to the teenager, "Bring in some young lovelies."

The boy got up with a groan and headed up the stairs.

Mustache man leered at Zita. "You know you'd fetch a pretty penny here. I can make you rich."

"No, thank you." She couldn't prevent the disdain on her face.

"Why, you rich enough?" He scowled. "You too good for us?"

Her heart thudded. She hadn't considered the gang might want her. She should have — it was what had happened to Teresa. Zita was saved from having to answer by the arrival of the lovelies. The girls trudged down the steps, all of them no more than teenagers. As Zita searched their faces for Manuela, all she saw was resignation or fear. Her heart wanted to burst. She wanted to save them all. They lined up in a row, and the man indicated to David that he could choose.

Feck. Manuela wasn't there. She couldn't say anything, could only hope David realized.

David took his time, standing in front of each one, checking them out and then moving to the next. When he reached the end, he frowned. "Got anyone younger? I'll pay well for a virgin." The expression on his face was creepy.

Zita translated and the man pursed his lips. "Virgins cost double."

When she told David, he said, "I've got the money."

The man ordered the girls out and said to the teenager, "Go get Manuela and Agatha."

Zita turned to the window as if she was bored so her relief couldn't be seen. Mustache man got to his feet and walked around to get a better look at Zita. Her pulse pounded. What was he going to do?

He reached out and caressed her cheek. She shuddered and stepped away.

"I'm not done with her yet," David said, moving to stand beside her. Zita translated.

The man looked at David. "Let me know when you are," he said in English. "I'd pay well to have her here."

David grinned and nodded.

Zita was so stunned she couldn't speak. She knew he didn't mean it, but damn he was convincing.

The boy returned with two young girls. One of them was Manuela, and she looked absolutely terrified, with tears welling in her eyes.

Zita wanted to smile at her, reassure her, but she couldn't. Instead she said to David, "Will either do?"

He slowly examined Manuela, a smile on his face. "She'll do nicely."

This time, she couldn't hide the revulsion on her face.

"You don't like it?" the man asked.

"Not my kink," she said.

"You like to dominate the women?" the man asked David in English.

David brushed Zita's hair out of her face to show the bruise. "Only when they need it."

The man nodded his approval. Zita was going to be sick.

David got out the money and put it on the table. "Will this do?"

The man took it and smiled. "Yes."

David took Manuela's arm and started leading her to the door.

Manuela sobbed hysterically, dragging her feet. "No, no."

Each cry ripped Zita's heart in two.

"Wait. Where the hell are you going?" Mustache man demanded and the teenager blocked their path.

Zita translated, her skin tight.

"I'm not taking my dick out in a place like this." The disdain on David's face was so much like Bob. "I'll catch something."

"He has a room at the hostel down the road," Zita added as she translated.

"It'll cost extra."

They negotiated a price.

"You'd better behave," the man told Manuela.

The little girl was shaking, but she nodded.

They took Manuela out of the building and one of the men on the door fell in step behind them. Zita wanted to tell her it was going to be all right, but she couldn't risk it yet.

When they arrived at the hostel, the guard checked out the room before letting them in. Tears streamed down Manuela's face. She reached out to Zita. "Please help me."

Zita couldn't bear it. She turned away as David shut the door with him and Manuela inside and the lock clicked.

"What's wrong, sweetheart?" the guard asked with a smirk. "Think you're missing out?"

Zita straightened. She had to remember why she was here; she had to keep this man distracted. "Not at all. He's not my type." She had to be careful. She didn't want to give him any more ideas than he already had. She had to be able to leave when she wanted to. "What about you? Don't you wish you had the girl?"

The guy grimaced. "I like women who know what they're doing." His eyes raked her body. "You'd know a thing or two."

She forced a smile on her face, hoping David would hurry up. "Well now, I don't like to kiss and tell." She stepped away from the door and he followed her, turning away from where David and Manuela would pass.

"I'm sure you don't," the man said. "Where are you from? I haven't seen you around here before."

"I'm from the other side of town," she said. "This guy needed a translator." Zita grimaced. "He didn't mention what he wanted to do."

"You following him around then?"

She nodded.

The man grabbed her. "Well, we could have a little fun of our own while we're waiting." He ran a hand down her arm.

She brushed him off, and as she did, Manuela and David hurried past. Relief filled her. "Maybe some other time. He gave me some errands to run and I don't want to be punished." She showed him her bruise. "But I'll be as fast as I can." She winked, blew him a kiss and hurried away, resisting every urge to sprint.

At the entrance of the hostel Zita checked if she was being followed. She wasn't. David pulled the car up and she jumped in the front seat. Manuela was lying on the back seat and she was no longer sobbing.

"*Niñita*, everything is going to be all right," she said. "We're going to get your Mama now."

Manuela nodded silently, tears streaming down her face.

Zita turned back to David. "Turn here." He did as she asked, and the laundry was ahead of them. The same guy was sitting on the step out the front. "Pull up there." She pointed to the curb. "I'll get Johanna."

"Be careful."

"I will be." Walking across the street, she breathed deeply and evenly to control her fear. They just needed to get Johanna and then they'd go home.

Johanna was serving a customer as Zita entered. There was a different man sitting on the crate out the back. The customer left.

"Johanna," Zita said. "Come and see this cute puppy outside."

Johanna's eyes widened when she saw Zita.

Zita smiled and gestured. "Quickly, you don't want to miss it."

Johanna hurried to the door and Zita followed her out. "The white car across the road," she whispered in her ear. "Manuela's in it. Go, get in."

With a shriek, Johanna raced across the road. The guy on the step yelled and stood. Zita shoved him and ran to the car as Johanna got in. David had the door open for her. She slid in and slammed the door behind her, her heart pounding. "Drive."

David hit the accelerator as gunshots rang out. The back window smashed.

"Get down," she yelled, as David swore.

Another couple of bullets hit the car before they sped around the corner and out of sight.

"Is everyone all right?" she called in Spanish.

"*Sí,*" Johanna replied, sitting up.

She turned to David and saw that the sleeve of his shirt was red with blood. Her heart stopped. "*Feck.* You've been shot." She slapped her hand over his wound.

He gritted his teeth and his hands were white on the steering wheel. "Caught some glass or something. Stings like a mother—"

"Pass me my backpack," she ordered Johanna. Both mother and daughter were clinging to each other, crying. "Now, Johanna!"

Johanna passed her the backpack.

"Before you do anything, does someone want to tell me which way to go?" David asked.

Zita couldn't remember. She translated and got the directions from Johanna as she ripped her skirt into strips. She pressed one bandage to the wound and David swore.

"Don't be a baby," she said, praying it was only a superficial cut. "Slow down," she said. "We don't want to get picked up for speeding."

He did as she said and she took the cloth away from the wound. It was a deep abrasion, like a bullet had grazed his skin. Her heart rate slowed. Taking another strip of cloth, she wound it around his arm. "We'll clean it when we get to the airport."

"Grab my phone and call Captain Johnson. Tell her we're on our way. We want to leave as soon as possible."

Zita dialed the number and organized the flight. Then she sat back, put her seatbelt on, and her heart rate came down to normal. They weren't being followed. She breathed in and out. The draft from the broken window was quite cool. "I don't think you're going to get your deposit back," she said.

David laughed and the sound lifted her heart. "I think you might be right."

***

It took a while to sort out the rental car and to clean David's graze, but once it was done, they cleared customs quickly and were settled in the plane by midday. Zita had called Carmen to tell her they were on their way home. Manuela still looked a little shell-shocked and Johanna hadn't stopped thanking Zita. But Zita wouldn't fully relax until they were in the air. They would definitely be safe then.

David had been silent the whole time. She was worried about him, but there was no privacy to talk.

Finally, the plane was cleared for takeoff and they were in the air.

When the captain announced they could now walk around the cabin, David said, "Zita, can I talk to you for a minute?" He stood and walked toward the bedroom.

She followed him. "What's wrong?"

He shut the door behind her and pulled her roughly into his arms.

"David?" She held onto him as he started to shake.

"Jesus, Zita. I don't want you to ever do that again." The anguish in his voice was clear.

Her heart melted as she rubbed his back. "It's all right. We're all safe."

His eyes were full of horror. "That place was hell. All those girls in there were miserable or defeated. How can those places actually exist in the world?"

She couldn't be angry with him. Not when he was so distressed. She kissed his cheek. "We're working on it. Fernando almost has enough evidence to shut it down."

"It's not right." Tears poured down his face. "Teresa was there, wasn't she? And Manuela . . . it could have easily been another man who'd hired her."

Zita held him tightly. She'd heard more than just Teresa's story, she knew these places existed, and while the reality of it had still been a shock, she had been prepared.

David hadn't. Not really. But he'd managed to keep it together until they were safe.

"You did so well," she said.

He grimaced, wiping the tears away and let out a deep breath. "I was not leaving that place without Manuela."

It would be best for him to talk about it. "What happened when you got into the hostel room?"

"She was terrified. She wouldn't come near me, wouldn't read the note you wrote, so I had to read it out to her quietly." He shook his head. "I'm taking Spanish lessons when I get home. I'm pretty sure I murdered the language, but she seemed to understand, particularly when I showed her the photo of Teresa. She climbed out the window and I followed. Then we waited for you."

Zita hugged him. "Thank you. I couldn't have done it without you."

"It was my fault you had to come. If I hadn't kept the damned file, if I'd listened to what my father was saying, rather than hearing what I wanted." He squeezed his eyes shut. "When Carmen told me you'd come here on your own . . ." He shook his head. "I was terrified I wasn't going to see you again." He reached for her. "I was stupid. Please forgive me."

Zita stepped away. She had to be clear, she had to explain. "I trusted you, David. I convinced my sisters to let you in, to share their stories with you. You broke not only my trust, but Beatriz and Teresa's as well."

"I know. I can't tell you how sorry I am."

She sighed. It wasn't his fault. It was Bob's. "I forgive you, but you need to apologize to Teresa and Beatriz as well."

"Of course. As soon as I get back." He took her hand. "Zita, I'm sorry I asked you to sit through that stupid dinner. I invited you because it was a family event, and for me that meant you had to be there."

What was he saying — that he considered her family?

"I love you, Zita, and I wanted my family to accept you, the way yours has embraced me."

Her breath caught in her throat. "What?" She sat on the bed.

He crouched down next to her. "I love you. I've known since Vegas and I should have told you right away."

The lump in her throat made it impossible to breathe.

"Say something, please, even if you don't love me." His beautiful eyes begged for an answer.

She loved him, but what would it be like the next time she saw Bob? Could she stand between David and his family? "What about your family?"

"What about them?"

"You love them. What if they won't accept me?"

He smiled. "I love that you'd consider them, that you'd worry for me." He was silent for a moment. "The only person who might be an issue is Dad, and after what he did last night . . . well, I don't care what he thinks any more."

Her heart hurt for him.

"I love you," he said again. "You're the only person I need in my life."

Her chest felt like it would burst. "I love you," she whispered.

"Say that again?"

"I love you," she said it loudly and he pulled her into his arms.

She held him tightly as tears rolled down her face.

"I'm so, *so* sorry, Zita for this whole mess."

"I know." She pulled back. "Everything is going to be OK." She kissed him.

She truly believed it would be.

***

By the time they arrived in Houston, Zita was exhausted. Her lack of sleep the night before and the adrenaline from the escape was overwhelming her.

It took a while to get through customs, as Manuela and Johanna's documents had to be checked, but finally they were able to head home. As they pulled up at Casa Flanagan, Teresa burst out of the house and raced over to the car. Johanna and Manuela scrambled to get out and they crushed together in a hug, tears flowing.

Zita's own eyes welled up as Carmen hurried over and pulled her into a hug. "You're safe." Carmen burst out crying and Zita held her.

"It's OK, Mama. We're all safe."

David pulled up next to them and got out as Bridget and Carly came running out of the house and joined the hug.

"What are you doing here?" Zita asked.

"We've been here all day waiting for news," Bridget said.

"Don't you ever scare us like that again," Carly admonished.

"Yeah. It's supposed to be me doing the heroic things." Bridget grinned, and then hugged her tightly.

Zita's eyes welled up as they let go of her.

Carmen pulled David into her arms next. "Thank you for keeping my baby safe."

"She did all the work."

"Come inside," Carmen said. "You must tell us everything."

They all crowded into the living room while Zita, Johanna and Manuela explained what had happened. They spoke in Spanish, but Zita translated for David, Jack and Evan, who were also there.

"I'm most definitely going to learn Spanish," David murmured into her ear as he drew her close.

She smiled. "I'm a pretty good teacher."

When the story had been told, they went to freshen up. Zita closed the bathroom door behind David and pulled him into her arms. "I haven't thanked you for helping me. Thank you for trusting me."

"You were so amazing, Zita." He kissed her. "Leaving you with that guy was the hardest thing I've ever done."

She wanted to erase the sadness in his eyes. "I can take care of myself."

"Yes, you can. But I'd like to take care of you too, if you'd let me." He looked into her eyes. "Marry me, Zita."

Her breath left her. "Really?"

"Really." He smiled. "I want to spend the rest of my life with you."

"What about your father?"

"I don't want to spend the rest of my life with him," David said with a smile.

"You know what I mean."

"He's not going to stop me from being with you. If he can't accept you, then we won't see him." He kissed her. "It's you I care most about. It's you I can't imagine my life without."

Zita hesitated. She hated to come between anyone, even Bob. "You need to be sure, David. I don't want you to resent me later."

"I've never been so sure about anything in my life."

She searched his eyes and saw his determination. "Yes." She smiled. "Yes, I'll marry you."

She shrieked as he picked her up and whirled her around.

Her year couldn't get any better.

Epilogue

Thursday evening, Zita arranged for her sisters, their partners and her mother to meet at Carly's apartment. Casa Flanagan had settled into a comfortable routine with their two new additions, with Johanna helping Carmen with much of the work.

Zita had received the DNA test results back and needed to tell them about Sean. She'd chosen a place away from home so Carmen had time to process the news. Johanna was with the foster girls.

As Zita unpacked the takeout she'd bought, Carly said, "Are you going to tell us what this is all about?"

Nerves swirled in her stomach. She was most concerned about how her mother would react. She glanced over at David who nodded. Taking a step away from the table, she said, "I discovered something recently, and with all of the excitement of El Salvador, I haven't had a chance to tell you about it."

Carmen immediately covered her hand with hers. "Did you not get into law school?"

"I'm not sure yet. It's something else." She gestured to the chairs. "You should all probably sit because it's going to come as a shock."

"Spill it, Z. You're freaking us out," Bridget said as she sat down next to Jack.

"A few weeks ago I investigated Papa's side of the family. I wanted to find out if we had any distant relatives."

"Your father's family is all dead," Carmen said gently.

Zita nodded. "I know that's what we thought." She swallowed. "I was searching through social media for Flanagans in Ireland and there was a profile picture of someone who looked so much like Papa." She showed them the photo. "I contacted him. I thought he might be a second cousin or something."

"*Madre mía.*" Carmen swayed in her seat and Bridget grabbed the phone from her to look.

Zita put a hand on her mother's shoulder. "His name is Sean, and he's our half-brother."

Carmen was already shaking her head. "No, no, no. Brendan would have never left his son behind."

"He didn't know, Mama. He left Ireland before Sean's mother knew she was pregnant." She told them Sean's story.

"You believe him?" Bridget asked.

"We both did a DNA test and the results confirmed there was a good probability of us being related. We'd get a more conclusive result if we could get Mama, and Papa's uncle tested."

"Where does he live?" Carly asked.

"Ireland." She let out a breath. "He'd like to meet us."

Bridget glanced at her mother and then across to Jack. "This is so strange, but I'd like to meet him."

Carly nodded. "Me too."

Carmen reached for the phone and examined the photo again, tears running down her face. She brushed a finger over the photo. "He's so much like my Brendan."

"I know, Mama. This must be so hard for you. I'm sorry."

She was quiet for a long moment and they all watched her. David put his arm around Zita and she leaned into him.

"Any child of Brendan's is welcome in my house," Carmen said finally. "I would like to meet him. We must arrange for him to come to Houston."

Zita let out a breath of relief. "He doesn't have any vacation time, but we can Skype with him."

"Maybe he could come for my wedding?" Carly said.

"Yes. He should come," Carmen agreed. "He is family."

"Speaking of family . . ." Zita smiled at David and said, "I have one more bit of news.”

David slipped his hand into his pocket and drew out a ring. Zita gave him her left hand as the squeals started.

“We’re getting married.”

ACKNOWLEDGEMENTS

A huge thank you to the people who helped me with this book: Ida from Amygdala Design for the beautiful cover, Dianne Blacklock for editing and Brooklyn Ann for proofreading. I must also thank Anne, Michelle and Carmen for helping me with my research.

Finally I really want to thank you, the reader, for reading Blaze a Trail. I really hope you enjoyed the story, and if you did, I'd love to hear about it. You could leave a review, or email me directly at claire@claireboston.com.

The Flanagan Sisters was always going to be a three book series, but then Sean came along, and well, I couldn't leave him without a story could I? Place to Belong, Book 4 in The Flanagan Sisters, will be out in January 2017.

About the Author

Claire Boston is the best-selling author of The Texan Quartet. In 2014 she was nominated for an Australian Romance Readers Award as Favorite New Romance Author.

Her debut contemporary romance novel, What Goes on Tour caught the attention of Momentum's Joel Naoum when her first scene was read aloud at the Romance Writers' of Australia (RWA) conference in 2013. This led to a four book contract for The Texan Quartet series.

Claire is proactive in organizing social gatherings and educational opportunities for local authors. She is an active volunteer for RWA, as a mentor for aspiring authors and the reader judge coordinator.

When Claire's not reading or writing she can be found in the garden attempting to grow vegetables, or racing around a vintage motocross track. If she can convince anyone to play with her, she also enjoys cards and board games.

Claire lives in Western Australia, just south of Perth, with her husband, who loves even her most annoying quirks, and her two grubby but adorable Australian bulldogs.

Claire loves to hear from her readers. You can find her at her website, www.claireboston.com, on Twitter, @clairebauthor, and on Facebook www.facebook.com/clairebostonauthor.

You can also join her reader group at **http://eepurl.com/Z4-4z.**

Break the Rules

The Flanagan Sisters # 1

Bridget Flanagan knows how to assess risks, but are the consequences of exposing her heart too dangerous?

Bridget has a passion for safety and in the world of oil refineries that makes her great at her job. So when her big promotion goes to someone else, she heads out on the town to forget her troubles. Jack Gibbs seems like the perfect man to distract her.

At least until Monday morning when she discovers Jack is her new boss. There's no way she's going to keep seeing him, no matter the connection between them. She's been burned before.

Jack can't understand why Bridget's so against their relationship. They positively sizzled during their one night together. He knows he has to be careful now she reports to him, but she tempts him in every way.

Can Jack convince Bridget to give him a chance, or is the risk too high?

http://www.claireboston.com/books/break-the-rules/

Change of Heart

The Flanagan Sisters #2

Software billionaire Carly Flanagan has an abundance of everything except time.

With everyone wanting a piece of her, or more accurately, her money, she spends her days trying to live up to her company's motto of Community, Sharing, Support. Having always been so focused on responsibility, success and supporting those less fortunate than her, Carly's forgotten to consider what she wants for herself in life – until she meets Evan.

Evan Hayes is an artist and free spirit, and when they meet at a local art exhibition, he is immediately intrigued by Carly. He sees through her public persona, realizing she is not the person she portrays. Evan's the type of man who doesn't have a lot, but is perfectly comfortable with who he is. A man who knows what he wants – and he wants Carly.

Carly is sure Evan wants something else from her. Everyone does. All Evan is asking is the chance to get to know her, but will Carly let him in? Or will a lifetime of protecting herself prove too hard to overcome?

http://www.claireboston.com/books/change-of-heart/

Place to Belong

The Flanagan Sisters # 4

Coming January 2017.

http://www.claireboston.com/books/place-to-belong